PAYBACK

Also by Fern Michaels . . .

FERN MICHAELS

PAYBACK

ZEBRA BOOKS
KENSINGTON PUBLISHING CORP.
http://www.kensingtonbooks.com

ZEBRA BOOKS are published by

Kensington Publishing Corp.
119 West 40th Street
New York, NY 10018

All Kensington titles, imprints and distributed lines are available at special quantity discounts for bulk purchases for sales promotion, premiums, fund-raising, educational or institutional use.

Special book excerpts or customized printings can also be created to fit specific needs. For details, write or phone the office of the Kensington Special Sales Manager: Kensington Publishing Corp., 119 West 40th Street, New York, NY 10018. Attn. Special Sales Department. Phone: 1-800-221-2647.

First Printing: September 2005
20   19

Printed in the United States of America

PAYBACK

Prologue

Myra Rutledge, heiress to a Fortune 500 candy company, looked around her state-of-the-art kitchen, at the pots bubbling on the stove, at the table set for two. Even though it was late afternoon, the sun danced through the stained glass ornaments hanging on the kitchen window creating rainbows on the white walls all around her. The girls—that's how she thought of Barbara and Nikki—had made the colorful ornaments for her as gifts one year at summer camp.

She'd adopted Nikki at a young age, but she and Barbara couldn't have been more alike than if they'd come out of her womb at the same time. Barbara was gone now, killed by a hit and run driver in the District by a man with diplomatic immunity.

Myra tried her best not to let maudlin thoughts overcome her, but sometimes, like now, at the end of the day, she thought about her two girls and the dangerous path she'd embarked on. She needed to fortify herself against such thoughts because she knew they weren't going to go away on their own. A snifter of brandy helped a little. She poured generously, eyes watering at the first massive gulp. She always gulped brandy even though she knew it should be sipped. She took another mighty gulp as she looked at the clock. The girls of the Sisterhood would be arriving before nightfall, to prepare for their second mission. The thought warmed her more than the brandy did. They were like daughters now, and she loved them all.

She was worried a little about Alexis, though. She'd mentioned her worry to her live-in companion, Charles, the way she mentioned everything that bothered her, and he'd agreed that perhaps Alexis *wasn't quite* ready for her mission. If not, they'd open the shoe box, fall back and regroup. It wouldn't be a problem. With Charles at the helm, it would all go smoothly.

There was another problem, though, outside of the Sisterhood. Assistant District Attorney Jack Emery, Nikki's fiancé. Ex-fiancé to be more precise.

Myra set the glass down on the table and massaged her temples.

"You're at it again, eh, Mom?"

Myra's head jerked upright as she looked around. One of the stained glass ornaments, a red tulip hanging in the window, was jiggling on its little hook. "Barbara? My dear, sweet girl, I was sitting here thinking about you and Nikki when you were little. I miss you so."

"I know, Mom, but I'm always close by. I'm looking at you right now. Don't worry so much. Things will work out. Trust Nikki."

"But Jack . . . Jack could ruin everything."

"Nikki won't allow it, Mom. I think what you're doing is super. That first mission of Kathryn's was really kick ass. Thanks, Mom. I know you're doing it for me, and I can't wait till it's your turn. I'll be with you every step of the way."

Myra looked down into her brandy glass. Was she really talking to her dead daughter? Was her dead daughter actually communicating with her? Or was it the brandy? She finished it off, not wanting to let go of her daughter's voice.

"Easy on the sauce, Mom. I'd hate to take away a vision of my mom dancing on the table. I know how rowdy you can get. I'm teasing, Mom."

"I know, dear. I'm feeling a little light-headed right now just talking to you. I wish . . . Oh, Barbara, I wish so many things."

"Don't, Mom. You can't un-ring the bell. I just

9

want you to know how proud I am of what you and the girls are doing. Sometimes . . . sometimes you simply have to take charge and make things come out right. Kathryn is a new person these days. You're right about, Alexis, too. She isn't ready, but Mom, let her be the one to tell you she isn't ready. Don't make the decision for her. And, Mom, just keep doing what you're doing."

"Oh, I will, dear, I will. I just thank God I have the money to fund this venture. And to think I don't even like candy."

"I hear Charles coming. I'm going upstairs to spend some time with Willie. I love you, Mom."

Myra smiled at the mention of Barbara's tattered teddy bear. "When Nikki moved back here to the farm she started to sleep with Willie so he wouldn't miss you so much."

"I know, Mom. Trust Nikki. And, don't worry about Jack. Nik has it under control. Love you, Mom."

Myra was up and off the chair in the blink of an eye. She ran over to the kitchen window to touch the stained glass ornament that was now still. Her hand flew to her mouth to stifle a sob.

She felt Charles's hand on her shoulder. She turned around to bury her head in his broad chest. "She was here, Charles. We talked."

Charles Martin, ex-MI6 operative who had devoted most of his life to Her Majesty, eyed the brandy bottle and the empty glass. "I'm glad, Myra. I'll finish up here. Why don't you check the bedrooms to be sure everything is ready for the girls. Did you buy something special for Kathryn's dog, Murphy?"

"Yes, Charles, I did, a chew toy and a box of jumbo biscuits. He's a wonderful animal, isn't he?"

"Yes, Myra, he is."

"I love you, Charles. I wish . . . I wish . . . never mind. Barbara said . . . it's all right, Charles. I'm not dotty. Isn't that a term you Brits use?"

"I'm an American now, dear. I say nutsy cuckoo like the rest of you. You are my dear, sweet Myra and I love you with all my heart. Scoot!"

Myra smiled. She adored flirting with the love of her life. "I'm going. I might have overcooked that mess on the stove, Charles."

"I'm throwing it all out, Myra, and starting over. It's all right, dear. You have other wonderful talents." He twirled the dish towel and then playfully swatted her backside.

Myra laughed all the way down the hall and was still laughing as she climbed the steps to the second floor.

One

Alexis Thorn frowned as she looked around her small apartment. There was nothing about the tiny place to suggest permanency of any kind. There were no knickknacks, no green plants, no family pictures. It was a place to sleep, a place to come home to at the end of the day, nothing more. How could it be anything else when her name wasn't even Alexis Thorn? Alexis Thorn was an alias. She'd taken a new name with the help of her lawyer, Nicole Quinn, when she got out of prison for a crime she didn't commit. She didn't want to think about why she was living in this run-down apartment but she had to think about it, like it or not.

Without Nicole Quinn she didn't know where

she'd be. Nikki had gotten her a job as a personal shopper to some of Virginia's older, wealthy residents. It was a far cry from being a high-powered securities broker in her other life, that was for sure. Nikki had helped her with a new identity, too. Who in their right mind would hire a jailbird? No one, that's who. These days she was Alexis Thorn and she liked it but someday when the time was right, she'd go back to being her real self.

Today, in just minutes, she had to climb into her little Mini Cooper and head out to McLean, Virginia. There at Nicole's adopted mother's palatial estate, she would join the other members of the Sisterhood. She'd joined a year ago, again, with Nicole Quinn's help. The Sisterhood wasn't just any organization. Myra Rutledge had formed the organization after her daughter was run down and killed by a diplomat's son. With the aid of Nikki's legal expertise, Myra formed the Sisterhood to help women get the justice and the revenge they deserved, even if it meant going outside the law to get it.

The Sisterhood consisted of six women, seven if you counted Myra, all recruited by Nikki. They'd gone on one mission so far and it had been successful. At the end of that successful mission, they'd drawn names to see whose case would be next. Alexis's name—not her real name of course—had been drawn from the cardboard shoe box.

But she wasn't ready yet to seek the justice she deserved. She needed more time to wallow in her misery, and to build up her strength and resilience. She didn't know why that was, it just was. She would have to tell the sisters they needed to choose someone else for the second mission. She knew in her gut she was still too fragile, too broken with her thirteen-month stint in the federal pen. She tugged at her lavender dress, straightening it over her slim hips. The dress was one she'd chosen from her pitiful wardrobe and was a knock-off to boot. It went well with her brown skin and dark hair. She'd chosen the dress because she thought she looked best in pastels. The days were long gone when she didn't think twice about buying high-end designer clothes. Everything from her past was gone. Every damn thing she cared about. Even her dog.

Alexis started to shake when she tried to imagine what the other sisters would say when she told them she wasn't ready for her mission. Kathryn, the most verbal, and the toughest of them all, in her opinion, would narrow her eyes and tell her to grow up and get with the program. Isabelle, who saw things other people didn't see, meaning, of course, that she was psychic, would shrug and close her eyes, maybe in the hope of conjuring up the reason for Alexis's pass on the mission. Julia, a retired plastic surgeon, who had contracted AIDS from her philandering husband, the senator, would stare at her as if she were a speck under a microscope. She'd say, "You need to make those bastards pay for what they did to you and get on with your life because you *have* a life to get on with." Yoko would nod and say she understood whether she did or not. Nikki would use logic to try to convince her to take the bull by the horns, and Myra, sweet, gentle woman that she was, would smile wanly and say, "Honey, if you aren't ready then you aren't ready and we'll choose one of the other sisters." At which point she'd feel like a fool and probably start to cry. The others would look at her with disgust and she'd cry harder. They might even become so disgusted with her they'd try to drum her out of the Sisterhood.

She'd done so well with Kathryn's mission. It couldn't have succeeded without her expertise. She could take nothing and transform it into something wonderful and exciting. She was a master with a makeup brush and she knew it. Costume design was something she loved doing. Nikki said she was a master at that, too. She'd been so proud when Nikki had said that. All the sisters had complimented her. Life after prison. She owed this new life to Nikki and the sisters. And she was happy. So, what the hell was her problem?

Alexis eyed her suitcase by the front door, and then let her gaze go to what the sisters called her Red Bag of tricks, complete with everything she needed to alter a person's being. Makeup, spirit gum, latex, costumes, wigs, glasses. She had the talent to take an ordinary person and transform him or her into a movie star. Where she'd come by this particular talent, she had no idea. Everything in the Red Bag had been updated or replenished by Myra.

Alexis looked at her watch. Time to get on the road. The Sisterhood's hosts, Myra Rutledge and Charles Martin, didn't like to be kept waiting. She smiled when she thought of Charles, Myra's right hand man, and the one who planned each mission. Charles was an ex-British MI6 operative who had once worked for the queen on the other side of the pond until he'd been compromised. In the spook world, according to Charles, the bad guys had found out who he was and steps had to be taken to keep him safe. Now he worked and lived with and for Myra. Charles always said being a super spy for Her Majesty had equipped him to head up the Sisterhood. On top of all his other accomplishments, Charles was a gourmet cook. Alexis felt her mouth start to water at some of the wonderful meals he'd cooked for all of them. Today, she hoped, would be something just as wonderful.

Suitcase in one hand, the Red Bag of tricks in the other, Alexis still somehow managed to lock the flimsy door of her apartment. She didn't look back because there was nothing to see except a bunch of shabby, secondhand furniture. She hadn't seen the need to buy new furniture, preferring to bank all her money until she was sure where she was going with her life. A new life, a new name without the stink of ex-con attached to it. What more could a girl want?

Alexis tossed her suitcase into the back of the Mini Cooper, then climbed behind the wheel. Before she turned the key in the ignition, Alexis looked around the ratty-looking neighborhood and the building she lived in. They should just demolish the entire three blocks. Once she'd lived in a pretty little house with window boxes and flowers on her front porch. She had furniture that she saved for, beautiful linens, fine dishes and crystal. And she'd had a dog she'd loved dearly. It was all gone now, sold to pay her legal fees. She'd been told that one of the officers who arrested her had taken her dog.

If anyone should be ready for revenge, it was she. She knew in her heart of hearts, deep in her gut, that the two partners who framed her for their own crime did it because she was a black securities broker. She'd been careful not to play the race card in her defense. Now, she wished she had. Maybe her problem was she couldn't come up with a suitable revenge that would make her whole again. Nothing she could come up with was bad enough, horrible enough, ugly enough to make her whole. Death was the only thing she could come up with but that wasn't an option. She had no desire to go to prison again.

Ever.

The engine of the Mini Cooper turned over and Alexis drove down the road to the highway. Another glance at her watch told her she had just enough time to make it to McLean. A smile tugged at the corners of her mouth. It would be good to see the sisters again.

As she drove away, Alexis noticed for the first time that spring had really arrived. The trees were dressed in their fledgling greenery and here and there she could see flower buds. Spring. A new beginning. She crossed her fingers the way she had when she was a child. Maybe this spring would be a new beginning for her.

As the miles ticked by, Alexis settled herself more comfortably in the driver's seat. She felt better already.

Myra Rutledge, Charles at her side, stood under the portico and watched as the cars inched their way through the open gates. Her smile rivaled the sun. "They're here, Charles! Every single one of them. I was so afraid they might have second thoughts. They look wonderful, don't they? I love the way they poke one another and make each other laugh. I am so relieved that they all get along just like real flesh and blood sisters."

Charles beamed. "Love, they are beyond wonderful. Julia looks particularly good, don't you think?"

"For now, she's in remission, but yes, she looks wonderful, just awfully thin. Look how they're all smiling, Charles. That means they're glad to be here. Turn off the power to the gate. We don't want any intruders today." Myra's voice dropped to a whisper when she said, "Nikki didn't say anything about . . ."

"No, Nikki didn't mention Assistant District Attorney Jack Emery at all. I didn't want to open any old wounds by asking. They broke off their personal relationship and Nikki is touchy on the subject of Jack Emery."

"A district attorney prowling around here with binoculars makes me worry, Charles. I know Nikki is still in love with him. I also know Jack Emery is not going to give up. He suspects that we were responsible for Marie Llewellyn's disappearance, a case that had nothing to do with the Sisterhood. He told Nikki so. That's why the two of them are estranged. They were on opposite sides of that case. He's trying to . . . to . . . get the goods on us, Charles."

Charles patted Myra's hand. "Not to worry, my dear. That will never happen. I want you to trust me."

Myra stared into Charles's bright blue eyes. God, how she loved this man, her daughter's father. "I do, Charles. I do. Now, let's welcome our new little family.

"Girls! Girls! Welcome back to Pinewood! Charles prepared lunch for all of us and we'll have it on the patio. Oh, how I've missed you," she said, opening her arms wide to gather all the young women close.

Murphy, Kathryn's dog, barked sharply for attention. Myra laughed. "You, too, Murphy. Charles fixed you a special treat." The big shepherd literally purred at her words.

Two

"Listen to them, Charles!" Myra said, pointing to the ceiling. "They sound so happy. This old place is alive again. I love to hear them laughing and poking fun at one another. And, did you see Murphy? I love the way he cozies up to you because he knows what a good cook you are." She paused, and a frown replaced her smile. "Things are going to work out for Alexis, aren't they?" she asked.

Charles Martin stared at the love of his life and smiled as he expertly turned over the shrimp fritters in the frying pan. Alexis's favorite food was shrimp fritters and since they were here to plot out her mission, it was only natural for him to cook her favorite food. On more than one occasion he'd boasted, shyly of course, that he'd personally prepared beef Wellington for the queen. He always followed up that statement by saying, *of course, that was in my other life.* "We'll just have to wait and see. Let her tell us. We'll take it from there." He hugged her.

"There's a glow about you today, my dear. You look like spring itself in your flowered dress. And"—he leered—"you smell heavenly!"

Myra patted Charles's hand. "Thank you, dear. Charles, how can I be so happy when we do . . . when we . . ."

"Make things come out right for our friends?" Charles said, finishing her question. "We committed ourselves, Myra, to right old wrongs, to settle old scores and to fight for those who fell through the cracks while the law was looking the other way. Let's not worry about the dark side today. You're happy, I'm happy, the girls are happy, and we're about to embark on our second mission. As they say in the business, 'I got it covered, lady.'"

Myra burst out laughing as she started to set the table. She looked down at Murphy, who was watching Charles's every move. "It's time for lunch, Murphy, fetch the girls."

Murphy raced to the bottom of the magnificent spiral staircase and barked, then raced back to the kitchen. Myra patted his big head and smiled. "He's a wonderful animal, isn't he, Charles?" Not bothering to wait for a response she said, "I feel so much better knowing he's with Kathryn when she drives that big rig of hers cross-country."

"Darling, you're jittery. Calm down. I hear them coming down the steps. For all our sakes, I want you to look and sound positive."

Myra held her regal gray head even higher. "Whatever you say, *Sir* Charles!" She smiled, referring to his knighthood. Charles grimaced. He hated discussing anything about his old life.

Charles beamed when the women swooped into the kitchen jabbering a mile a minute.

Myra hugged them one at a time before they all sat down.

"Shrimp fritters! My favorite soul food," Alexis said.

Yoko reached to the middle of the table and said, "The tulips are real! They are so beautiful! My own at the nursery are just starting to bud."

Isabelle shaded her eyes with her hand and said solemnly, "I *see* acres and acres of tulips and they're all purple . . . I see . . . ."

Kathryn turned in her seat and swatted Isabelle. "Then, oh mighty seer, you must be in Holland, you jerk!" Everyone laughed at Kathryn's reference to Isabelle's clairvoyant capabilities, which were iffy at best.

"Spring is my favorite time of year," Nikki said as she shook out her linen napkin. "The tulips are gorgeous. Are they the ones Barbara and I planted when we were little?"

Myra squared her shoulders, her eyes bright at the mention of her dead daughter. "No, dear, those are long gone. These are a new variety. Charles and I planted them last year. The colors are remarkable so that means the seed catalog didn't lie. The golden yellows are my favorite. Barbara loved the shell pink ones and those are just starting to bloom."

Julia, her eyes as bright as Myra's, said, "I don't know about the rest of you but I am so glad to be here. I feel . . . I feel like I've come home. I don't mean to sound maudlin or anything but I feel like you're all my family. So, let's make a toast to the Sisterhood."

"Hear! Hear!" Charles said, raising an exquisite crystal pitcher of sweet tea. He poured it into matching goblets before he took his seat at the table. As one, the women raised their glasses. Charles did the honors and said, "To all of us. To the Sisterhood and their lone brother!"

Myra was the first to burst out laughing. "That's my Charles," she said fondly. "Now, girls, let's devour this wonderful luncheon Charles has so lovingly prepared so we can get to work and do what we do best: going after the scoundrels who have turned your worlds upside down, so we can give you back your lives."

Midway through the meal, Murphy reared up next to Kathryn and let out a bloodcurdling howl. The women looked at one another in alarm. Kathryn got up and went to the kitchen door and opened it. Murphy raced outside, the hair on the back of his neck straight up. Nikki got up and followed Kathryn. "Easy girl, easy," Kathryn said, placing a hand on Nikki's arm. "It might be a squirrel or a rabbit. It doesn't have to mean it's Jack Emery out there spying on us."

"Yes, it does, Kathryn. He's been stalking me when I go into the city. I never see him but I know he's there. He's on a mission now just the way we are. He's got himself convinced we all helped to spirit Marie Llewellyn away after she killed the man who murdered her only daughter. He's never going to give up, that's why he's such a good district attorney. I hate to say this but he's better at tracking than a herd of bloodhounds. He's out there somewhere watching and waiting. I'd stake my life on it."

"Then I guess it's time we did something about Assistant District Attorney Jack Emery," Kathryn said flatly. "Come back to the table, Nikki, we can't let Charles's dessert go to waste."

Myra's voice was hushed when she asked Nikki, "Is it . . . ?"

"Jack? Yes, I think so, Myra. I think he's been stalking me. I also think he's got some of his people watching the rest of you, too. I don't know where he's getting the manpower unless he's calling in favors from his friends and they're doing it pro bono. D.A.'s do that all the time. Let's face it, he's got us staked out. We have to find a way to work around that or else we have to ... do something drastic where he's concerned."

Dessert suddenly lost its appeal. Charles cleared the table and the women got up to help him. Kathryn went back outside. They could hear her whistling for Murphy.

Myra's back stiffened as she walked over to the kitchen door. "I hate it that people are spying on us. I'm going to call the K-9 Kennel in town and have them bring guard dogs out here to patrol the grounds at night. They do that, you know. They bring them late in the afternoon and the dogs patrol all night. Their handlers pick them up in the morning. I read about it in the Sunday section of the paper a while back. A lot of companies are doing that these days because they don't want to risk their employees getting shot during a robbery. That's not to mean they don't care about the dogs, they do. The dogs wear Kevlar vests and it's very difficult to shoot at a moving target."

"I think it's a good idea," Charles said, turning on the dishwasher. "Myra, take the girls to the war room and I'll make the call. I'll join you shortly. I'll have Murphy stand guard when I get ready to join you."

Myra led the way through the house to the library where she stepped in front of a solid row of bookshelves. She counted down the various carvings on the intricate molding that ran the length of the bookshelves. At the same moment her fingers touched the lowest carving, the wall moved slowly and silently to reveal a large room with wall to wall computers that blinked and flashed as well. A mind-boggling, eye-level, closed-circuit television screen was focused on the security gates. Each wall seemed to be made up of television screens. MSNBC was playing on the south wall, CNN on the north wall and the FOX news channel was playing on the east wall. Fans could be heard whirring softly. There were no windows.

They'd all been here before in the command center and knew that Charles had installed a modern day ventilation system. He had also installed a cutting-edge, solar powered electrical system. If the weather took a turn for the worse, there was enough stored power to last a month.

The women waited for Myra to secure the door before they took their seats at a large round table surrounded by deep comfortable chairs. The only thing on the table was a Keds shoe box and a stack of bright yellow folders at Myra's place.

When Myra joined them the women made small talk as they waited for Charles to join them. No one, it seemed, was interested in going to the Cherry Blossom Festival in Washington over the weekend. Nor were they interested in inspecting the new drainage and sprinkling system Myra said she had installed last month. They were saved from further mundane conversation when the door slid open and Charles entered the room.

"Six K-9's will arrive for duty at five this afternoon. All right, ladies, we're ready to discuss business. If anyone has a question or a problem, aside from the problem of Jack Emery, let's hear it now before we get down to work."

Alexis took a deep breath and raised her hand. "I'm not ready," she said. "I thought I was but I'm not. I've done nothing but think about this the whole past month and I can't come up with a suitable punishment for the people who framed me and sent me to prison. Well, that's not exactly true, I did come up with something but it's death. I don't want any of us to be responsible for a murder. So, I want to give up my mission, for now, to one of you."

Kathryn tugged at the sleeve of her flannel shirt. "Alexis, are you sure? I felt the same way when my mission was called first. Don't you want to talk to us about it? Maybe we can come up with something."

"Yes, I'm sure. I want to be the one to come up with a punishment. I was the one who sat in a federal prison for thirteen months. I haven't come to terms with it yet. Please, can we pick someone else?"

Myra looked at Charles and then let her gaze sweep around the table. "Raise your hand if you agree to cancel out Alexis and move forward with a new mission." Seven hands, including Myra's, shot in the air. Charles raised his hand at the last second.

"It's unanimous, then. Obviously, these are not needed now," Myra said, indicating the yellow folders that contained all the information the Sisterhood would need for Alexis's mission. "We'll need some additional time to plot out a new mission once we choose a new sister. Can you all return here in, say, three days? You're welcome to stay if you like. Perhaps I'm getting ahead of myself. Let's choose a name first," Myra said.

Everyone watched as Charles scribbled names on small pieces of paper, put them in the shoe box, then shook it vigorously. Isabelle did the honors and picked a slip of paper. She handed it to Myra.

Myra smiled as she read the name. "Julia Webster!"

Julia's clenched hand shot in the air. "Unlike Alexis, I am soooo ready! However, I wonder if I might request a two part mission. The one has nothing to do with the other but the reason I'm asking for this favor is . . . when . . . if I'm no longer here, you might want to consider replacing me with the person I want helped." Julia bit down on her lip, her eyes filling with tears. "Welcome her to the Sisterhood . . ."

Kathryn, who was tough as nails and meaner than a snake, slid her chair closer to Julia to put her arms around her. "I'm for whatever you want, Julia, and you're going to be with us for a long time. Tell us what you want."

Julia cleared her throat and spoke sharply and clearly. "I want my husband to suffer. I want him disgraced and destroyed for what he did to me. I want his face plastered all over the front pages of the newspapers. I want his colleagues to look at him with disdain and disgust. I want him destitute. I don't care if he has to live on the street and sleep in a cardboard box.

"The second part of my mission deals with a colleague of mine. She's an oncologist and has to deal with people who can't get the medical care they need because their HMO refuses to authorize the proper treatment. There is one HMO in particular that a good majority of her patients belong to, actually three HMOs under one umbrella and owned by the same family. My friend's name is Sara Lang and we've known each other since college. We roomed together. In many ways she's like a sister. She's at the end of her rope and talking about giving up on her profession. I just want to tell you about one patient of hers. It was a little nine-year-old girl with leukemia. Sara found a bone marrow donor for . . . for . . . Emily. The HMO wouldn't pay for it. The family, the grandparents, were broke. There was no place left to borrow. No place for them to go for help. Emily died last week. They all die! All her patients who have that crappy HMO die. Do you hear me, they fucking die!

"Now let me tell you about the family that owns the three HMOs. They have billions of dollars. That's billions with a B. It's a woman, her husband and her son who run the company. They're worse than those Enron and WorldCom people who cheated all their employees out of their pensions. They know every politician in Washington on a first name basis and that includes my husband. They throw parties, donate to causes if it gets their name mentioned or their picture in the paper. They are on every party list in town. I want them punished. I want it so bad, but if we can't do a two-part mission then I want to give up my personal mission with my husband. I'll just . . . kill him myself. What do I have to lose?"

Exhausted, Julia fell back in her chair.

The silence in the room was broken only by the whirring of the overhead fan. When Charles cleared his throat the sound was so loud, all the women jumped.

"I personally don't see a problem if the others agree. However, I'll need more than three days to pull all that together. Can we meet back here one week from today? If I manage to get everything together sooner, you'll be notified. Now, who wants to leave and who wants to stay?"

Kathryn elected to leave to do a run to New

Jersey with a load of Florida oranges and grape-
fruits, promising to keep her cell phone on the
entire time. Julia said she would go home, gather
all pertinent papers and return, assuring everyone her husband wouldn't even know she was
gone. Yoko had a husband and couldn't stay.
That left Isabelle, Nikki, and Alexis who would
stay and help Charles.

Outside in the bright spring afternoon, Myra
gathered Julia in her arms. She felt so thin, so
fragile. "We'll make it all come out right, dear. I
wish I had known, I would have helped."

"Those bastard companies have to be made
to pay. Maybe it will make the other HMOs sit
up and take notice. I don't want to see Sara give
up her career. She's one of those rare doctors
who cares about her patients. She uses all her
own money to help. She lives in a hovel if you
can believe that. She's just too tired to fight anymore, Myra."

"It's now our problem, Julia. We'll take care
of it. Hurry back but drive carefully."

"Myra?"

"Yes."

"He doesn't deserve to live. But I don't know
if I really have the guts to kill him."

"Shhh. We'll take care of Senator Webster."
Myra bent down and picked a bright red tulip
from the border along the walkway. She handed
it to Julia who smiled.

Myra waved as the women climbed into their

vehicles and drove away. Murphy barked from the passenger seat as Kathryn's big rig sailed through the gates.

Myra stood where she was for a long time, her eyes scanning the dense foliage that surrounded the house. Somewhere out there, Jack Emery was watching her. She could sense it, feel it. She shivered, not with cold but with fear.

Three

It was a balmy sixty-nine degrees outside; the women had been chattering about sunning themselves later if time permitted. Charles held up his hand for everyone to quiet down. He found the instant silence gratifying.

Today, a stack of green folders sat in front of Myra. "I think we can dispense with the formalities and get right to business," Myra said as she handed out the folders with Julia's case outlined in detail.

"What you have in front of you is the life history of Senator Mitchell Webster as we know it. Unfortunately, there really isn't all that much information so I'm hoping Julia can fill in the blank spots. Julia?"

Julia quickly scanned the loose sheets of paper and appeared stunned at what she was reading. "I don't see anything here about Mitch's childhood." Julia laughed bitterly at her own words. "His childhood, his background, was created by the very high-powered marketing firm, Johnson and Powell. You do stuff like that in the political game. I guess it's more glamorous."

"That particular firm certainly falls into the big league. I've heard of them," Charles said. "Julia, you need to explain exactly what the firm created in regard to your husband. Tell us everything you know even if it doesn't seem important."

"You mean besides creating a monster?" Julia shook her head. "I don't know where to start. It was so long ago. I was just starting medical school in New York when I first met Mitch. He could've sold me the moon and stars I was so awe-struck by him. I was twenty-two. He was thirty-four, an older man. I was flattered that he even talked to me, even more flattered when he asked me out for coffee. The rest, as they say, is history."

"He was a junior senator. What was he doing on a Manhattan college campus?" Nikki asked.

"He was giving a speech. I was just one of hundreds who skipped class that day to listen to him. Being a junior senator, he felt the need to distinguish himself from all the other junior senators as well as the senior senators. He liked to be noticed. He needed a *cause*, something that would get him singled out by the media, his peers, it didn't matter who or what it was, just as long as he got noticed.

"In the mid-eighties, the hot topic was abortion. That was Mitchell's ticket. Women's rights and abortion. He couldn't have picked better causes. Both were hot button issues. He was young, incredibly handsome. Women gravitated toward him. I was one of those liberated, pro-choice flunkies who hung on to every word he said. When he was in the paper, I read about it. Hell, I even clipped the articles and started keeping a scrapbook. When I learned he was giving a speech at Columbia, I was ecstatic."

Charles looked at Julia, a frown building on his face. "What was so horrible about his past that made him feel he had to reinvent himself? Was he afraid of something? Or maybe someone?"

"It's a long story," Julia said.

"We're not going anywhere, dear. We've got all the time in the world," Myra said in a soothing voice.

"I know, it's just that *I* don't have all the time in the world."

"I think you should start at the beginning, dear, just like we did when we were preparing to take care of Kathryn's problem. Charles, please turn the recorder on."

Julia licked at her dry lips and took a sip of water before she started her story.

"It was in the fall, around the first of November, the first time I met Mitchell. We met a few times after that, just going for coffee, that kind of thing. He appeared to like me because he called quite often and we'd talk. I had this really weird feeling that he had checked up on me and knew my family was wealthy. He never mentioned it, though. Each time I would try to find out about his background, he'd change the subject and say things like, 'What you see is what you get' or 'I'm an open book.' His evasiveness bothered me so I did a check on him myself. Nothing jumped out at me right away. He wasn't close to the people he left behind. And, no, I never did meet any of Mitch's family."

"Never?" Myra said.

Julia shook her head. "In a way it really didn't seem important. I was in medical school, Mitch was in Washington 'running the country' as he put it. We were lucky we could meet up twice a month. I knew there was something wrong but I didn't want to pry. Remember, I was in love. I was also young and impressionable.

"Anyway, I managed to get a little background on Mitch, just enough to scare me out of my wits. If what I found out was true, Mitch should be in prison. He'd been involved with a young girl who was later found dead. Mitch then disappeared, according to what I was able to find out. I thought there had to be a mistake and there were two Mitchell Websters. You don't get to be

40

a senator without a thorough background check. I convinced myself Mitchell was who he said he was. I let it go. Years later when DNA became well known and used, it turned out Mitch hadn't killed her after all.

"Mitch and I got married a year later and moved here. I put his name on all my bank accounts and brokerage accounts. We were happy. At least I was. I never, ever, dreamed he was . . . seeing other women. I suspect now that he was an alley cat from the beginning. I was so busy . . . he was so busy . . . We had our weekends. That's what our marriage was for many, many years. Weekends. Then even those dropped away because Mitch was always going somewhere. He moved up, sat on more prestigious committees and became very high profile. I was busy with my patients. We still had sex once in a while, but the last three years of our marriage became strained. Mitch started staying away for days at a time, but he was mysterious about it. He said everything he did was on a need-to-know basis and he couldn't talk about it. I'm sad to say I believed him.

"When I had my physical I found out I was HIV positive. I was so numb with shock I didn't know what to do. I went to the Hay-Adams and checked in for a week to try to get myself together. I took three more blood tests, all with the same result. The only way I could have contracted HIV was through Mitch. I checked and double-checked each and every one of my surgeries. None of my patients had HIV. I had no mishaps in the operating room. Mitch gave it to me." She paused and looked around the table. Nobody moved a muscle. Everyone was looking at her, waiting for what she would say next. She took a sip of water and got her emotions under control.

"And now I want my pound of flesh. If you could rip his skin off at the same time, I'll accept that, too. I'm sure he doesn't even suspect that he's infected. If they don't do a full-blown AIDS check, HIV can go unnoticed. He would never believe he could contact such a violent disease. He simply wouldn't allow it."

Charles spoke first. "What kind of background did the firm create for Mitchell?"

"Everything that's public knowledge. His parents died, he had foster parents who put him through college. I think he has a sister somewhere who he pays to stay out of his life. I heard him on the phone one time but I never put it together until much later. At this point, I'm not even sure I heard what I heard. I'm not sure about anything anymore," Julia said sadly. "I guess my point is, no one in the media came up with anything on his background; his phony background. I find it strange."

Charles handed a box of tissues to Myra who then handed it to Julia. She wiped her eyes. "Was I an idiot or what? I can't believe I was so naive." She looked at the other women. She saw nothing in their expressions except sympathy and a new hatred for the man she was married to.

"So, where do we start?" Nikki asked Charles. "I know you still have connections at the White House, but are they secure?"

"Yes, but I don't think I'll need to use them just yet. We have several options. It's up to Julia to decide."

Julia looked around the table at her friends. "I want the bastard to suffer, and I want it to happen gradually. Mitchell believes he is invincible. It's going to take a lot more than a threat from me to bring him to his knees. He's a master at covering his ass. That means no matter what I come up with, he will have a pat answer. He'll turn the whole thing around and accuse me of having an affair. He'll say it often enough that he will believe it. Whatever you do, do not forget how powerful he is. His friends are even more powerful."

The group of women nodded. "What about his past? You said his entire background was phony. Can we actually prove it?" Charles asked Julia.

Julia laughed, a bitter sound. "Yes, and no. The problem is getting the right people to listen, and believe me, Mitch has spent most of his adult life on the Hill. He has lots of friends in Washington. Friends who owe him favors. Some of those friends are on the . . . scummy side. Mitch won't hesitate to call all his favors in if he thinks I'm going after him," Julia said.

"Tell me about his past. The real story," Charles insisted. "The story he doesn't want his adoring public to hear."

Julia nodded. "You'll probably find this hard to believe, but Mitch has no idea I know about his past."

"How did you find out and manage to keep it from him? I don't know if I would be able to keep quiet about my husband's past; if I knew he did something terrible I'd want to confront him," Nikki said.

"I lost count of the times I wanted to confront him but something always held me back. I'm afraid of him. He has a lot to lose and he wouldn't think twice about . . . letting me ruin his life. I want to think I was supposed to save this information to use at the right time. Now is the right time. The world is in bad enough shape without people like Mitchell Webster controlling it."

"Go on," Myra urged. "I want to hear what that horrible man has gotten away with. And to think I would have voted for him if I'd lived in Pennsylvania."

Julia smiled wryly. "He sucked you in too? Don't feel bad, Myra, it's what he does best. He's sucked in the whole state of Pennsylvania with that phony background he made up. He lied. He had sex with a girl who was later murdered.

"For starters, we all now know Mitchell is HIV positive. That in itself would blow his image all to hell but not enough to ruin his career because he'd find a way around it. He could say he was infected when he donated blood. He would come out the victor, I have no doubt. So that alone isn't enough to damage him permanently. And I want my vengeance to be permanent. I don't want to see the bastard resurface five years later. He may not even have five years." Julia paused. "I may not have five years left myself. I do have enough time to see that Mitch gets what's coming to him. All I need is your help in planning his destruction." She looked at Charles with hope in her eyes.

"You already have our support. What we need to do right now is decide in what order we're going to start dropping tidbits of information to the public," Charles said. "First, I think we should start by revealing his phony past anonymously to a few of the tabloids. Those vultures run with everything. Let Mitch go to war with them. Give him a few weeks to lie low, let the dust settle. Then, we move on to the next wave."

"Which is?" Julia questioned.

Charles spoke up. "You realize you will be in the public eye with him, don't you? Next, I think you should reveal that you suspect Mitchell is being unfaithful. But let it out accidentally. Better yet, let one of your friends do it for you. Would Sara, the oncologist, help you out here? We want your image to be that of a heartbroken wife who stands by her man." He heard several groans. "Scratch that thought. I'll come up with something better."

"I'm sure Sara will help. I will be more than happy to play the scorned wife. You know, there was a time when I first learned about Mitch's cheating, that I *was* heartbroken. After the fifth or sixth time, I didn't care anymore. I had my career, I was happy with that. If Mitch needed me at his side for some political function, I was there. I wonder how many times his colleagues were laughing at me behind my back. I guarantee Mitchell's cronies knew he was a cheating bastard." Tears formed in Julia's eyes. "You know what bothers me more than anything?"

"What, dear?" Myra asked, sensing Julia needed an older woman, a mother image, to listen and empathize with her now.

"Being laughed at. It enrages me to think about all the women he's had affairs with. I'm sure some of those women are the wives of his good old 'Capitol Hill buddies.' I wonder what those good old Capitol Hill buddies would do if they suddenly learned Mitch had affairs with their wives."

"I think I can find out everything you want to

46

know. I, too, have friends on *the Hill.* We could use the information later if we need to. It couldn't hurt to have Senator Webster's cronies by the . . . short hairs," Charles said bluntly.

"Yes. I can give you names of some of the wives I've suspected over the years. Linda Cromwell for one. Her husband is Senator Cromwell from Delaware. She called the house several times when Mitchell didn't think I was home. I picked up the extension and listened to their phone conversation once. They weren't talking about politics."

Myra flinched. "And I thought Mrs. Cromwell was such a prim and proper lady. Very school-marmish. I saw her on *Face the Nation* the other day with some other senators' wives. They've formed a committee of some sort," Myra said. "I might be wrong but I think it had something to do with pediatric AIDS."

Julia nodded. "You're not wrong, Myra. The wives scheduled a fund-raising dinner for next week, five thousand dollars a plate. The proceeds will go to their newly established foundation. I can offer my help if you think it's a good idea."

Nikki beamed. "I think it's a wonderful idea but let's not decide just yet. If the senator's world starts falling apart, he's going to place blame on the person he's closest to. That person is you, Julia."

Julia nodded. "Yes, I suppose you're right.

There is something else. After Mitchell and I were married I insisted his name go on all my accounts. Damn, I already told you that. I'm sorry. I'm starting to stress out about this. I haven't seen any bank statements for months. I don't know if that means anything, but he does have access to my money. What does that have to do with anything, anyway?"

Charles bit down on his lower lip. He didn't like the sound of this and it showed. "I want you to close out your accounts immediately. For your sake, Julia, I hope there is something left to close out. Can you do it without Mitchell finding out? You didn't do anything with your trusts did you?"

Julia swallowed hard and shook her head.

"That's good, at least you have money coming in. We might want to take a look at those trusts later on."

"I don't foresee a problem. The accounts don't require both signatures. I can do it first thing tomorrow."

"Good." Charles said. "The rest of us will be acting behind the scenes as much as possible. Tonight when you get home, act as if nothing has happened. Don't say or do anything that you wouldn't normally do."

"What about my leave of absence from the hospital? I went to Nicole's office to have her review my new contract with the hospital a while ago and to ask her advice. At that time I was still trying to figure out a way to stay on, perhaps as a consultant. We both decided it was a good idea to just take a leave of absence for now and not renew the contract. I had Nikki draw up my resignation papers but I haven't turned them over to the hospital nor did I mention it to Mitchell because . . . Nikki advised me not to. And as you all know, that's how I learned of the sisterhood. Nikki seemed to think I was a good candidate. I don't want Mitch to suspect I'm not working. I am a doctor and he might wonder why I'm not going to the hospital. I can't keep going shopping every day, which is what I've been doing. Not that Mitch checks up on me but there is a first time for everything. Do any of you have any ideas?"

"Have you taken a leave of absence before?" Myra asked.

"I've taken time off when Mitchell was running for office. I went on the campaign trail with him for a few weeks. Other than that, no."

"Let me ask you this, does Mitchell confide in you? Would he tell you about Governor Cartwright asking him to be his running mate if he decides to run for the presidency? Those rumors are floating all over the District."

"He confides in me about certain things. Yes, I think he would tell me about that. I think it's just a rumor that Mitch started himself. He likes to gloat too much not to tell me. This is just my opinion but I've always thought he felt inferior to me. Don't ask me why. He's been a senator for sixteen years now. I suppose it could be my money. I've thought for years he resented me because of it but it doesn't stop him from spending it. Yes, I think he would tell me about the nomination, just to rub my nose in it. It's just a rumor at this point. Isn't it?"

Charles held up the latest edition of a smarmy tabloid and pointed to the headline that said, "Webster on Crawford's short list." "Then you have your answer. Don't tell him you've taken a leave of absence until he tells you about Crawford. After he tells you, wait a few days, *then* tell him you'll take a leave of absence to help him with his campaign."

"I can do that. Yes, I think it will work. I have to go to the hospital and clear out a few things in my office. I'll take a day longer. Mitchell doesn't keep close tabs on me anyway. He's never had a reason to."

"Now, Julia, tell us what you know about Mitchell's past. Everyone, take notes. I've got the recorder on, but notes are an extra precaution. Just in case. One of you might pick up on something the rest of us miss," Charles said, pointing to the high-tech recorder that was no bigger than a cigarette lighter.

Julia took a deep breath. This was harder than she'd thought it would be. When she'd learned she was HIV positive, her world had come to a crashing halt. Getting even with the bastard she was married to was the only thing that kept her going. Now that it was time to get down and dirty, she wondered if she had enough guts to make it happen. She didn't want to place herself in the same category as Mitchell and his Capitol Hill cronies, but if she didn't stop him, he would keep lying, seducing women and spreading a disease that would be the death of everyone he touched.

"I'm ready," Julia said as the others prepared themselves to take notes.

"Just start out telling us what he told you. Then you can tell us how you found out he lied," Charles instructed.

Julia nodded. "I always knew Mitchell's 'public' family history. I never had a reason to question it until after we were married." Julia twisted her hair around her finger, a faraway look in her eyes.

"Sorry. I was . . . this is harder to talk about than I thought."

Myra smiled gently. "Take your time. We understand what you're going through, Julia. You're human. You are about to destroy a man you once loved," Myra said.

"We married in November, almost a year to the day after we met. I was in love and all was right with the world. However, when the holidays rolled around I asked Mitchell if we would be going to Virginia to spend the holidays with his family. I still hadn't met them and I thought

51

they'd want to meet their daughter-in-law. Mitchell got angry and told me he was estranged from his family. He said when he was ready for me to meet them, he would see to it that I did. I pretended to understand. Some families don't get along. Two years went by and I still hadn't met Mitchell's family. By that time I knew whatever was wrong had to be something more than a family dispute."

"Two years is a long time to wait," Alexis said.

"Yes, two years is a long time but I was in medical school and didn't have a lot of free time, so I didn't give the matter too much thought. Mitchell was busy running for another term at the time, we were both wrapped up in our careers. Christmas rolled around again. I asked Mitch if he was going home for Christmas and he blew up. He threw a few plates as I remember. We were having dinner together for a change. I guess I thought it was the right time to ask about them. It wasn't. I realized then there would never be a right time to discuss Mitch's so-called adopted family. I let it go. For weeks I thought about hiring a private detective to track Mitch's parents down. Turns out the father drank himself to death and the mother had the same addiction and died shortly after. I found out what the real argument was all about. I debated a few months, thinking it wouldn't be in the best interest of my marriage to send someone digging into Mitch's past. Of course I got over that after I convinced myself Mitch gave me no other choice. He was being dishonest and I wanted to find out why." Julia paused for breath, then took a pen and started to scribble on a yellow legal pad.

"When I found out I was shocked. I couldn't believe how Mitch had fooled the voters. To this day I don't understand why a tabloid hasn't homed in on this information and made it public. They feed on stories like Mitchell's. If he does run with Cartwright, they'll turn him inside out. Mitch and his public relations experts, if you want to call them that, said Mitch was adopted by a well-to-do Virginia family when he was thirteen, after spending thirteen years in and out of foster homes. I guess that was supposed to make him appear more sympathetic to his voters. I was his wife. You would've thought he would at least tell me the truth."

"They say the wife is always the last to know," Nikki mumbled.

Julia agreed with a nod and continued. "Finally, I hired a private detective. One of the best in New York City. Mitchell had his career. Despite all of my concerns, I didn't want to cause trouble for him. Of course what Mitchell didn't know wasn't going to hurt him. I was overly paranoid. I guess I thought whatever my detective discovered he'd go public with it.

Which, fortunately for me, and for Mitchell, never happened." Julia looked at the women. She had their undivided attention.

"Mitchell's adoption story was a lie. He was never in a foster home until he was sixteen. Evidently it was hard to place him at that age. Mitchell lived with his mother until he went to live with the Websters."

"If he wasn't adopted, how could he use their name?" Myra asked.

"He had his name legally changed when he turned eighteen. The Websters took him in when he was sixteen, then sent him to college. He was like one of their own, but they never formally adopted him. And they were not well-to-do by any means. Mrs. Webster's name is Lavinia and she worked in a grocery store. Her husband, Carl, worked for the state. They were a hard-working couple. They never had children of their own. Mitchell filled that void for a while. Both of them died in a car accident in the early nineties. Voters do not like to be lied to."

"And you never confronted him with this information?" Charles asked her, his voice registering shocked surprise.

"Never," Julia said flatly.

"This detective told you all of this?" Nikki asked in a plaintive voice. She looked at Myra as she shook her head.

"Yes. I have the report in my office. I never brought it home for fear Mitchell would find it.

I didn't want him to know what I'd done. I felt in some crazy way that I had betrayed my husband by checking up on him."

"I can't believe a man with the senator's power and position in the Senate hasn't been exposed for the phony he is. I would bet my last dime that Senator Webster spends big bucks to keep his past out of the papers," Nikki said as she looked at Julia. "If I were you I would get my finances in order. If you have anything left to get in order."

"Mitchell's life is about to fall apart, isn't it? And I'll be the one to bring it crashing down. He'll kill me if he ever finds out what I've done."

"Then we have to make certain your husband never finds out, don't we?" Myra said to the room at large. "It goes without saying, this conversation is never to leave this room."

"When do we start to leak this to the press?" Alexis asked. Relief at being out of the spotlight shone on her face.

"Shortly," Charles responded as he scribbled on his own yellow pad.

"Be warned about Mitchell. He wants to control everything and everybody around him. He told me once that he loved the power being in the Senate gave him. He said he had the power to screw up lives if he wanted. Then he laughed. He thinks it's all about him. And it is. If marrying Mitchell Webster is going to be the death of me, I'd at least like to know before I die that the son of a bitch suffered too," Julia said vehemently.

All the women in the group centered their attention on Julia. If any one of them had a right to revenge, it was Julia. She would die because her husband was unfaithful. Her death, whenever it came, would not be in vain. The Sisterhood would see to it that Senator Mitchell Webster suffered before his death. Nikki would see to it personally.

Charles looked at the group of women. "Nothing that was said in this room today should be repeated. Not to your husband, your best friend or even your dog. You never know who might be listening. We must be very careful. This time we're not dealing with a gang of bikers or insane neighbors. We are going to be up against the federal government in a sense and I for one know what they're capable of. You don't want to find out the hard way. Let's call it a day. I will see you back here day after tomorrow at seven A.M. Does anyone have any questions? Is there anything else you want to add, Julia?" His voice was so kind, Julia found herself smiling.

"Well, there is one other thing. For any of you who are *really* interested, Mitchell has the American flag tattooed on his ass."

Charles choked and looked away. Kathryn guffawed and slapped her leg. The other women just tittered.

Kathryn managed to stifle her laughter. "What about the rest of us, Charles? Are we going to sit by and watch you have all the fun?" Kathryn asked.

Charles fixed his gaze on Kathryn. "I'm surprised you asked, you have barely said a word this morning. Yes, I have something for all of you to do. You're not going to get off that easy." He smiled at her and wiggled his eyebrows at the same time. Yoko, Isabelle, and Alexis laughed.

"As we know, Alexis is a master at disguise, having learned the art in college and Little Theater work. If the need arises, and I'm not sure at this point if it will, you will do what you do best with your big Red Bag." He watched as she slid her notes across the semicircular table in front of her.

Charles looked down at his own scribbled notes. He held up his hand. "I made some changes since we're going to be running a dual mission this time around. Tell me if it's going to be a problem."

" Do I stay or leave?" Alexis asked.

"You can leave, but remember, be back in forty-eight hours." Charles admonished.

"Yes, sir!" She saluted quietly before she walked out the door.

"Yoko, you will assist Kathryn. I'm quite comfortable saying you both are going to be quite busy. I have a contact at Governor Cartwright's mansion in Maryland. They are in charge of decorating the armory where Jefferson Cartwright plans to announce his running mate. It's a good guess it will be Senator Webster. They will want floral arrangements for all the tables as well as the stage where the podium rests. I'm thinking somewhere around five hundred arrangements. Can you handle this, Yoko? That means no delivery of oranges to New Jersey for Kathryn. We're going to need her rig."

A look of panic settled on Yoko's face. "How do I explain all of this to my husband?"

"I don't think you'll have to explain anything, Yoko, I rather imagine your husband will thank you for securing such a large flower order."

"I can do a lot of things, but arranging flowers isn't one of them," Kathryn grumbled good-naturedly.

"And you won't have to learn, my dear. As it stands, Yoko and several of you will have one van for deliveries. It wouldn't do for Yoko to borrow the van as he will need it. It would take all day just to load the flowers and drive them to Cartwright's headquarters. With your semi you can do it in one trip. You'll be helping to unload the flowers. Our friend Mr. Emery may be watching so it will all seem quite natural."

"How can you be so sure Yoko will get the flower order? What a silly question." Kathryn grimaced as she remembered how Charles had pulled strings and arranged her mission down to the last detail. When one had powerful friends in powerful places as Charles did, anything could be accomplished.

Charles's voice rang with confidence, leaving little doubt that he could do what he said he would do. "Leave the details to me. If I say it will happen, it will happen.

"Isabelle, you will be working here at Pinewood with Myra. Nikki will assist me here in the war room. At this point it may seem like a walk in the park but don't be fooled. We're about to destroy a man's political life as well as his personal life. We have to be extremely careful so that we don't destroy our own lives in the process."

When the war room door closed behind the women Charles sat down in Myra's chair and looked around. His insides started to kick up a fuss at what he was contemplating on behalf of the Sisterhood. This was so unlike Kathryn's mission. This mission could, if not conducted properly, land all of them in prison. During his long and distinguished career in Her Majesty's Secret Service he'd been comfortable with his role of super spy because everyone he worked with knew his or her job. Their very lives depended on one another. The women of the Sisterhood were in no way professionals but they were women and in his opinion, women had an edge with their intuitive senses. Not that he would ever admit that to anyone except perhaps Myra, the one true love of his life.

His mind raced in all directions. He had to sit and think quietly to find the best way to conduct this new dual mission with a minimum of risk for the women he now thought of as his family. He looked around at what Myra called his lair. Everything in this room was state-of-the-art, so high-tech no one but government agencies knew about it and here it was, sitting in a secret room in Pinewood. Of course this could never have happened without Myra's wealth. When she said money was no object, she meant money was no object. His stomach crunched at the millions he'd spent in outfitting this room and she hadn't blinked an eye. He knew she would spend every last cent of her vast fortune to avenge her daughter's death. *Their* daughter. He couldn't wait for the day it was Myra's turn to be vindicated. That mission would be a mission of love with the Sisterhood.

Charles looked down at his watch. He chewed on his lower lip, something he did when he worried, and he was worried about Jack Emery. Strong measures might have to be taken where Assistant District Attorney Emery was concerned. How that would affect Nikki was something he didn't even want to think about.

* * *

From his perch, high in an oak tree, Jack Emery trained his binoculars on the vehicles leaving the Pinewood compound. He watched as the women hugged one another before Dr. Julia Webster climbed behind the wheel of her brand new Mercedes. Even from this distance Jack thought she looked thinner than the last time he'd seen her. She also looked pale to his trained eye. He shrugged; women were forever dieting.

Kathryn Lucas, the truck driver, was next. The huge black dog hopped into the cab and settled himself while Kathryn talked to the Asian woman. They hugged, too. Lucas left first in the rig and then the Asian woman followed her. That left the tall, long-legged African-American beauty. He watched until the Mini Cooper sailed through the gates. He could hear the clank of the gate closing from his perch high in the tree. He had operatives waiting along the stretch of highway to follow the women to wherever they were going.

That left Nikki, the Flanders woman, Myra Rutledge and Charles Martin, Myra's major-domo.

When Jack was sure there would be no further outdoor activity, he climbed down from the tree, dropping to his haunches. Something was going on, he was sure of it. For one thing, two visits by all the women in two weeks was one visit too many. Then there was the addition of the six

Doberman dogs that arrived at five o'clock every afternoon and stayed through the night. Yes, something was definitely going on.

Jack dusted off his jeans as he started toward his car. He was so damn tired. How much longer could he keep this up? He was lucky to get three hours sleep a night. He knew he was obsessed with this place, these women, and Nikki in particular. Long ago he'd learned to pay attention to his gut instincts and those gut instincts said these seven women were up to their pretty necks in something covert. And whatever it was, Myra Rutledge was bankrolling the project.

He knew that somehow, some way, Myra and the women had managed to spirit Marie Llewellyn, her husband and children to a place of safety. He'd prosecuted that woman for killing the man who had killed Myra's daughter. He hadn't wanted to do it but it was his job. The law was the law. He'd looked like a fool to his superiors when he couldn't figure out how Marie and her entire family dropped off the face of the earth on a wild, stormy night. To this day, there was not a single clue as to what happened. Nikki knew what happened, he was sure of it.

Jack opened the door of his car, climbed in and started the engine. His cell phone was in his hand a second later as he called his operatives for reports.

Damn, he was so tired he could hardly hold up his head. When he turned the power off on the cell phone he started to think about Nikki. He knew in his gut he was one of those guys who would only love once. Nikki was that love. He should never have given her that ultimatum. Ultimatums never worked. Someone always won and someone lost. Nikki had chosen Myra over him. It was the bitterest pill he'd ever had to swallow.

Four

The war room buzzed with the hushed voices of the women seated at the table. Charles, busy on the computer, only half listened to their conversation. What he was doing right now was solidifying the plans for Julia's revenge. He was tired but exhilarated. He'd called in favors from other retired operatives who were only too glad to offer their expertise in their chosen field. He held up his hand and shouted to be heard over the fax machine that was spitting out paper at the rate of twenty-six pages a minute. Overhead the television monitors came to life.

Charles stood high above the floor on a specially built dais. The king of all he surveyed.

When he had the women's attention, he pressed a button on the huge monitor next to where he stood. The scales of justice came into view; Lady Justice in all her glory lit up the room. As always, when the women saw Lady Justice they became subdued.

"First things first. I want to apologize for the late hour," Charles said, motioning to one of the clocks hanging on the wall. It was eleven o'clock in the evening, time for the late news. The sound was muted. He would turn up the volume in exactly ten minutes for the sound bite he wanted the sisters to hear. Now, though, he spoke quickly and concisely.

"Nikki has returned from Lynchburg. I thought it wise to send her on a scouting mission to make sure our facts are on the money. You'll all be given a copy of her report. I regret to say that Senator Webster is not responsible for Janet Bradshaw's death. Julia already told us that but I didn't want to leave anything to chance. Nikki and Julia both spoke with the young girl's mother. There is no point to going into detail. DNA doesn't lie. Senator Webster did have an affair with the young girl but he was not the father of the child she was carrying. Yes, the man is a philanderer. Yes, he has a shady background. But he did not kill anyone. I want to be sure we're all clear on the matter. Nikki was unsuccessful in locating any stray members of the senator's real family. What that means to all of us at the moment is the senator gave himself a make-believe background which in itself is not really a crime. What he did to Julia is the crime. We need to be clear on that.

"That leaves us with Julia's immediate problem. We cannot turn the senator over to the authorities for manufacturing a phony background. Millions of people do it every day. The fact that the man is a United States senator does, however, make a difference because that means the man duped the very people who put him into office. Will that matter? I doubt it.

"All we can do now is go after Senator Webster for what he's done to his wife. And to other women we don't know about at this point in time." Charles held up his hand for silence as he turned up the volume on the huge television set. "Listen!"

The evening news anchor looked gleeful when he said, "Just hours ago we received Governor Cartwright's short list for his running mate in the presidential race. Heading the list is Senator Mitchell Webster. What was up to this point an unsubstantiated rumor has now been confirmed. Channel Five tried to reach the senator for comment before airtime but we were unsuccessful." Charles turned the volume down.

"Well, that's never going to happen!" Julia shouted. In a lower tone, she said, "Is it, Charles?"

Myra reached across the table to pat Julia's hand. "No, dear, that is not going to happen."

Charles took up his usual position behind Myra's chair. "We have five days before Governor Cartwright's party where he will make his announcement. We have one foot in the door with the flowers. What that's going to get us is not quite clear yet but I am working on it. Julia will, of course, be there along with her husband. Our first leak to the tabloids will hit the paper the day before the event, the second, the day after the event when the senator is on a roll.

"Now, this is where it's really going to get interesting. The Monarch family, owners of the three HMOs we discussed previously, will be at the party. What that means is all three of them will be at their mansion in Manassas prior to the event. At the moment they're in their other mansion up in Peekskill. They're due to arrive in town tomorrow or the day after."

"Oh, Charles, hurry and tell them the best part," Myra said, excitement ringing in her voice.

Charles laughed, a robust sound. "Myra received an invitation to attend the party. If she had opened last week's mail last week, we would have known sooner. Now, what that means to the Sisterhood is this. You're all going to attend. We're creating new identities for all of you. You'll be considered heavy hitters with pockets full of money. The only thing politicians love more than themselves is people with money. Alexis, with her magnificent bag of tricks, will alter your appearance so you don't look like yourselves. Simply put, you'll be going in disguise. Myra has ordered exquisite fashions for all of you. And, as I said, Julia will be there on the arm of her husband."

Kathryn slapped the table with the palm of her hand. "Way to go, Charles!"

"Then what happens?" Nikki asked.

Charles waited a minute before he spoke. "Then we snatch them all!"

"Oh, girls, don't you just love the way that sounds?" Myra bubbled.

"Kidnaping is . . . it's . . ." Isabelle struggled for the proper word.

"Against the law? Well, of course it is. So was slicing off those guys' balls who raped me but we did it anyway. What's a little kidnaping charge?" Kathryn growled.

"Then what? Where? How? Details, Charles, details," Nikki said.

"All in good time. We have five days and I will need every bit of that time to fine-tune everything. As you all know, the devil is in the details."

Julia raised her hand. "What will we do with them when we . . . snatch them? Do you have even a vague idea of where we'll take them?"

"The revenge is yours, Julia. You and the others have to decide what their punishment is to be. I'm just your backup. I think you all might need the five days that are coming up. The one thing you can count on is that the location will be secure."

Charles walked back to his station. He returned with an armful of stapled bundles. "What this is," he said, handing each woman a document, "is the list of all the Monarch HMO subscribers. It's a bit mind-boggling at first, but go to the summary at the end where I've listed those claims that were denied, the deaths of the subscribers due to denial of claims, pending cases, closed cases. It's all broken down by age groups. The last page is Monarch's P&L sheet. You might want to keep those numbers front and center when you decide on the family's punishment."

Kathryn was the first one to bellow, "This is outrageous!"

"Scum of the earth," Nikki said.

"It's pitiful," Myra said.

"I didn't know it was this bad," Julia said.

"We should kill them all," Yoko said heatedly.

"Killing them is too good. They need to be punished and I do mean punished. They need to suffer," Alexis said angrily.

"I think we're ready to adjourn for the evening, girls. Let's head for the kitchen and some nice hot cocoa. Charles, would you care for some cocoa?"

"Not right now, Myra. I have hours of work ahead of me. We'll meet again in the morning at eight-thirty."

They were a somber group as they meandered around the kitchen getting in Myra's way as she tried to prepare the hot cocoa. When Nikki's cell phone chirped, their gaze whirled to the clock over the stove. They listened as Nikki clicked the on button.

"Hello," Nikki said quietly.

"Nik?"

"That's my name. What do *you* want? Do you know what time it is?"

"Of course I know what time it is, it's almost midnight. Guess your Tiddly Wink game is over for the night or are you guys having a sleepover? Kind of old for that kind of thing, aren't you, Nik? What'd you go to Lynchburg for? Never mind, I already know. When is everyone going to leave?"

"You sneak! You're spying on me, aren't you? I'm going to file a harassment charge against you, Jack. Don't call me again, either."

"Come on, Nik. You know you love me. I know what you're doing. Give it up before I have to arrest you."

"I'm not doing anything but playing cards. If you want to make an ass of yourself by trying to

71

arrest me, go ahead. I'll fry your ass and I won't need any help doing it either. You'll be the one who gets arrested. You're out there, aren't you, you son of a bitch! I bet if I went outside and waved you'd see me, wouldn't you?"

"Why does Myra suddenly need six vicious Dobermans, Nik? What kind of gig are you women running out there at ye old farm, *Nik?*" His voice was so sarcastic Nikki shivered.

Nikki sucked in her breath. Her heart started to pound in her chest. "We aren't running any kind of gig out here and the reason Myra got the Dobermans is to keep people like you off her property." Without waiting for a reply, Nikki clicked the off button.

The women clamored for an explanation at the angry look on Nikki's face. She stuttered and sputtered until she got every word of Jack's phone call out.

"So what you're saying is Jack is *on to us,*" Julia said.

Nikki gulped her hot cocoa and then bellowed when she burned her throat. Her eyes watering, she gasped, "What it means is, he *thinks* he's on to us. Yeah, he's on to us."

Yoko, the gentlest, the quietest of all the women, started to pace around the kitchen table. "Then we have to . . . eliminate him, is that not right?"

Kathryn slapped Yoko on the back. "God,

we're corrupting you, Yoko. What's gotten into you? You were a pacifist when we first met!"

Yoko squared her slim shoulders. "He's spying on us so he can send us to prison. I do not like that. That's what they do in countries where there is no democracy. And, he's broken Nikki's heart. Now he's threatening all of us. We have to do something!"

Myra spoke in a soothing voice. "Our plates are rather full right now, Yoko. I don't see how we can . . . perhaps we should invite Mr. Emery for tea."

"Mr Emery doesn't sound like a reasonable man, Myra," Alexis said. "We can't let him keep doing what he's doing, which is spying on us. Eventually, he's going to nail one of us. I'll kill myself before I let anyone send me back to prison."

"Shhh. You aren't going back to prison," Nikki said. "I'll take care of Mr. Emery. You know, Myra, inviting Jack for tea isn't such a bad idea."

"What will we do with him?" the new Yoko demanded.

"We could have those vicious dogs guard him," Julia volunteered. "Yes, I think that's a viable solution. But, that means Myra will have to make arrangements for the dogs twenty-four seven. Perhaps we should vote on it."

Nikki's mind raced. Did they dare snatch Jack? She looked around at the women. She saw panic and anger in their faces. Even Myra looked . . . disturbed. But tea? Yes, Myra would invite him for tea but would Jack take her up on the invitation? For some reason she didn't think so. Jack was out for blood. Still, it was worth a chance.

"Should we do it, dear?" Myra asked. "I think we should . . . what's that saying police officers use all the time? Oh, yes, chop him off at the knees. That's what we need to do. Should we tell Charles?"

"Absolutely we should tell Charles," Nikki shot back. "I'll do it now."

"More cocoa, girls?"

"No!" the women chorused.

"Then why don't we all smoke a cigarette. Does anyone have a cigarette?"

"No!" the women chorused.

One by one they trooped out of the kitchen, muttering a good night as they passed Myra's chair. Left alone with her thoughts, Myra's shoulders slumped. Her eyes filled with tears. Jack Emery couldn't be allowed to compromise what they were doing. He just couldn't.

Myra got up and reached into the cabinet over the sink for the bottle of brandy she kept handy for medicinal purposes. If ever there was a medicinal moment, this was it. She didn't bother with a glass but upended the bottle and took a hearty gulp. Her throat burned and her eyes started to water. She took another huge gulp before she corked the bottle and set it back in the cabinet. She tottered to her chair and plopped down. She started to cry. "Oh, Barbara, honey, I think I might be failing you. If Jack catches us, all this will be in vain. I only set this whole thing up to avenge your death. Now, it's more than that. I want to help the others, too. What a silly old woman I am to think I could make this all happen. Just a silly old woman."

"Mom, there's nothing silly about it. Stop worrying."

"Barbara, is that you? Darling girl, talk to me. Are you at peace? I think about you every day. I miss you so. The others have made my loss bearable, but now with Jack out there somewhere," Myra said, waving her arm in the general direction of the back door. "I don't know if we can hang on. Nikki's living here now, you know." Dear God, she was babbling to her daughter's ghost.

"I know, Mom. I'm glad she's here with you. Trust her. She can handle Jack. I have to go, Mom. Nikki and Charles are coming back to the kitchen. I love you, Mom. Mom, lay off the sauce, OK?"

"Where are you going, honey?"

"Upstairs to cuddle with Willie for a little while."

A wild *swoosh* of air circled Myra and then the kitchen was still.

Nikki stood in the doorway. She, too, felt the

75

swoosh of air. She knew instantly that Barbara had paid a visit to her mother.

"Talk to you later, Nik."

Nikki knew when she went upstairs to bed that Barbara would be sitting in her old rocker with Willie in her lap. They'd talk like they did sometimes about everything and anything.

Charles stopped in his tracks. "Was that . . ."

"Yeah," Nikki whispered.

"Oh."

Myra looked up, her lips trembling, her eyes moist. "I think I'm going to go to bed. I had . . . What I mean is, I drank some brandy. Maybe it was a lot. Is everything all right?" she asked as an afterthought. "Oh, would you like me to make you both some hot cocoa?"

"Good God, no, Myra. You make terrible cocoa," Charles said.

The heiress to a Fortune 500 company sniffed as she got up from her chair to go upstairs. "So what if cooking isn't one of my strong points. I have other talents, don't I, Charles?" She giggled like a schoolgirl as she sashayed past Nikki who did her best to hide her smile. Charles's ears turned pink. Myra whirled around and almost fell. "Should I wait for you, dear?"

In spite of himself, Charles chuckled. "Is that an invitation, Myra?"

Myra drew herself up to her full height. "Damn straight it is, Charles."

This time, Nikki did laugh aloud. "Go!" she said. "Before she kills herself going up the steps."

Nikki sat for a long time at the kitchen table. She felt like the weight of the world was on her shoulders. What was she going to do about Jack? If they snatched him, the D.A.'s office would start to look for him. Appealing to his sense of decency was not an option. Jack was a bull dog with the instincts of a bloodhound. And he was angry with her. That alone was motivation enough for him to want to put the screws to her and the others. She wondered how much he really knew and how far he was willing to go to nail all of them.

Nikki fished her cell phone out of the pocket of her slacks, turned it on and dialed Jack's number. A cell phone ringing in the woods. How funny was that? She almost laughed when a vision of the ADA, sitting high in a tree, his binoculars trained on the house, appeared before her.

Jack picked up on the first ring. Nikki figured it was lonely in the woods. "So how's it going out there in the piney forest, Jack?"

"I'm not in the piney forest," Jack said.

"Liar! You're up in a tree spying on us. You aren't the only one with high powered binoculars. We've got the night vision ones. You know the kind where everything looks green. You get yours at Radio Shack?"

"Smart ass! I'm home in my living room."

"Liar! I'm calling to invite you to tea tomorrow." When there was no response, Nikki said, "Well?"

"You must have me mixed up with someone who would be impressed with an invitation to Pinewood for tea. You know I hate tea."

"OK, coffee. What? You're afraid of me all of a sudden?"

"Hell, no, I'm not afraid of you. The woman hasn't been born who can scare me. I don't trust you or Myra. By the way, I've got a dossier on all those fine women visiting out there all the time. A real mixed bag, Nik. The bunch of you are up to something. I can smell it, and you know damn well I have excellent instincts."

Nikki sucked in her breath. Her hand holding the phone to her ear was shaking. "So, is that a no or a yes?"

"Like I'd allow myself to get within ten feet of you, counselor? Did I say I don't trust you?"

"Yeah. Yeah, you did say that. Ten feet, huh? I remember when we were molded to each other. You were my second skin if I remember correctly, but that was when you loved me, right?"

"Get off it, Nik. I'm not going down that road. Don't think you can sucker me in with an invitation to a tea party. I gotta go, time for bed."

Nikki snorted. "Be careful you don't fall out of your tree, there, Mr. ADA."

"You're a hateful woman, Nicole Quinn, and yet I still love you."

Nikki looked at the dead phone in her hand and started to cry. "And I still love you, too, Jack."

Five

Charles served breakfast on the patio to a group of somber, sleepy-eyed women who also looked angry.

"Ladies, ladies, how can you look so glum on such a beautiful spring morning?" Charles asked as he held the wrought-iron chair for Myra who was all smiles this morning. His voice dropped to a whisper. "Voices carry," he said, waving his arms to the thick forest that surrounded Myra's estate. "Generalities, ladies."

Nikki looked toward the piney forest wondering if Jack was still out there. She couldn't help but wonder if Jack really did have some hightech equipment that would allow him to overhear their conversation. She struggled for something to say. "The patio flowers are so pretty this year, Myra." The others, taking their cue from her, concurred.

Myra was still smiling. "Lu Chow, the gardener, brought them over yesterday. They look like a veritable rainbow, don't you think? I'm thinking I should dispose of this overhead sun umbrella and get one of those retractable awnings. Yes, I've made up my mind. Isabelle, dear, can you design something so that it doesn't look new? You know, have it blend with this old farmhouse?"

"Of course. What color would you like?"

"Green and yellow. Outdoorsy, if you know what I mean."

And so the conversation went until the girls cleared the table and trooped back inside. Myra closed the patio doors and drew the blinds.

A whispered conversation followed as Charles instructed Julia to drive back to Georgetown. "It's imperative that you find out as much as you can from your husband. If possible, you can return here this evening or tomorrow. Once Crawford makes his formal announcement that your husband will be his running mate, the Secret Service will move in and you will be under a microscope."

Julia looked stricken. "I never thought of that, Charles. How . . . what . . . I'll be a liability to all of you if that happens."

"No, you won't dear. Charles will figure out

something. This is your mission and nothing is going to stop us from carrying it out, not even the Secret Service. Now, do as Charles says, put a happy smile on your face and go home to talk to your husband."

"Today is Saturday. Mitch plays golf on Saturday. He might not be home. I see problems already."

Charles placed a comforting hand on Julia's arm. "There will only be problems if we don't act as a group. When you get to your car, use your private cell phone and call your husband. Be firm when you tell him you must talk with him today. I think he'll cancel any plans he might have to talk with you. He needs you now. And the press will be buzzing everywhere. I've taken the liberty of writing out some instructions for you. Peruse them when you make a stop at the hospital to pick up your shopping list of possible drugs we might need. You won't get another chance to go to the hospital again before we begin our mission." Seeing the panic in Julia's face, he said, "Julia, you can do this. I wouldn't ask you to do this if I didn't think you were up to it."

Julia drew a deep breath and squared her shoulders. In a jittery voice she said, "Of course I can do it. I won't let you down. I guess I should be going. I just need to get my bags." She looked around. "You know, in case anyone out there in the woods is watching us."

One by one the others volunteered to go with Julia. Charles just shook his head. "Trust me, Julia will be fine."

They all walked Julia to her shiny black Mercedes. They waved and laughed as Charles instructed. Julia waved back, a sickly smile plastered on her face.

During the drive to Georgetown, Julia gritted her teeth, repeating over and over, I can do this. I will do this. I have to do this. She reached down for her cell phone and hit the button on her speed dial that would connect her with her husband. She was stunned when she heard her husband's voice.

"Mitch, it's Julia. I'm on the way home and I need to talk to you. Please wait for me. I really don't care if you have a tee time or not, Mitch. I need to talk with you." She listened to her husband's litany of excuses. Suddenly she was sick of it all, sick to death of her husband and sick to death of knowing this was the man who was responsible for giving her a death sentence.

When he finally ran out of reasons why he couldn't wait for her, Julia said, "Listen to me very carefully, you son of a bitch. You need me. I do not need you. You either wait for me or I'll give an interview to the press and I won't be shy about mentioning what an alley cat you are. And you'll be attending Crawford's announcement party by yourself. How will that look, Senator? Now what's it going to be? And,

Senator Webster, I want to know what you did with all that money you took out of my account, which by the way, I closed out yesterday. You *will* wait for me, Mitch."

Julia hit the end button and turned off her phone. Let him keep hitting his own speed button till his damn finger fell off. That was almost funny because she knew her number wasn't on his speed dial because he never called her. If and when he did call, it was one of his aides with a message. She struggled to remember the last time she'd had a phone conversation with her husband but in the end she gave up. What did it matter now?

In the parking lot of the Georgetown Hospital, Julia read Charles's instructions three times until she had them committed to memory. Her eyebrows shot up once and then twice at the impressive list. Charles was right, she'd never get another chance to do what he wanted after today. When she was sure she had everything clear in her head, Julia tore the list into little pieces and stuffed them in her pocket. Once inside the hospital she would throw the pieces in different trash containers.

Julia, brisk professional that she was, made no stops on her way to her old office. Inside, she ran Charles's shopping list over in her mind as she opened and filled her medical bag. Her task completed, she looked at the sorry-looking philodendron on her desk. She wondered why no one had watered it. Maybe, like herself, it was meant to die. Like hell.

Julia grabbed the plant and raced down the hall to the kitchen where she used a plastic fork to stir up the hard earth. Somewhere in one of the cabinets there was a bottle of plant food one of the nurses had brought in. Six drops to a plant was what she'd said. Julia watered the plant, soaking it thoroughly before she added the six drops of plant food. With a paper plate underneath the plant she made her way back to her office where she set the plant on the desk. With a pair of old surgical shears, she trimmed off the yellow leaves. The plant still looked sickly and half dead. Just like me, she thought. Julia remembered reading somewhere that you were supposed to talk to plants to make them thrive.

Julia muttered and mumbled as she looked through her desk to see if there was anything else she needed to take with her. At the last second, she opened the drawer and took out all of her prescription pads and jammed them into her medical bag.

Done.

Julia was just about to walk through the emergency door exit when she stopped and ran back to her office. She reached for the plant and smiled. "You still have six leaves, my friend. That's not a death sentence." She stopped in the kitchen and took the bottle of plant food and left a ten dollar bill with a note in its place.

Now, she could leave this place. In her heart she said good-bye because she knew she'd never be coming back.

Fifteen minutes later, Julia entered her house in Georgetown carrying her plant. She set it on the kitchen counter, then turned to face her husband. Mitch Webster roared like a lion as he stormed about chastising her for making him wait when he had a golf date with the House Speaker.

"Ask me if I care, Mitch. I don't. Did you make coffee? I need a cup. Would you like one?"

"No, I don't want any coffee. What the hell's gotten into you, Julia? I just heard you took a leave of absence. Why?"

"I felt like it. Overwork, you know," Julia said as she scooped coffee into the plastic container. She turned to look at her husband with clinical interest. He was still a handsome man, tall and lean, exquisite tailoring, just the right tan to his face. He must use a sunlamp, she thought. His nails were manicured. She hadn't noticed that before, either. Just the right amount of gray at his temples to make him distinguished. Beautiful, dove gray eyes, thanks to artificial lenses. Capped teeth that had made some dentist happy. A good-looking man who shared her house, and a senator to boot. She wondered why she didn't feel anything.

"Congratulations, Mitch! You should have told me."

"They told me not to say anything. You knew I was on the short list. It was in all the papers. It's a whole new ball game now, Julia."

"You bet it is. Well, guess what, I don't want to play in that ball game, Mitch. The reason I wanted you to wait for this little talk was to tell you I want a divorce. I also want to know, down to the penny, what you did with all the money you took out of my account. Close your mouth, Mitch, you look like a hooked fish."

"What the hell's gotten into you, Julia? You can't divorce me. Not now. I'm going to be the next vice president of the United States."

Julia sniffed. "I hope you don't expect me to be impressed, Mitch, because I'm not. I have no desire to live in Washington's fishbowl. Being a senator's wife was bad enough. I'm surprised you're so willing to give up your senate seat. Being a vice president will be incredibly boring. All those funerals you have to attend. You'll have to give up your tomcatting ways because every move you make will come under scrutiny. Like I said, I want a divorce."

"Julia, Julia, Julia. I can't believe what I'm hearing. We're an old married couple. We're going to grow old together. That's what we promised each other when we got married. Look, I know we more or less lead separate lives these days but that's what this fast paced life is all about. You have your career. I never interfered with what you wanted to do when you wanted to do it. I tried not to make demands on you. I know how you hate politics. But for Christ's sake, Julia, this is the vice presidency. I could even be president some day."

"Don't grovel, Mitch. It's very unbecoming. You made a fool of me with all those women you chased around with. I know about them all. This whole town has been chittering about you for years." *I should tell him now that I have AIDS. Why am I so unwilling to say the words aloud? I should be sticking a knife in his gut for what he's done to me. Charles said this wasn't the time.*

Mitch's face lost some of its color. "I'm not going to deny it, Julia. But, I was discreet. It's your fault. You were never home. You never wanted to go anywhere or do anything. You turned into some old frump. And let's not forget how tired you always were and how many headaches you had. What was I supposed to do? You need to take your share of the blame for that, too."

"I'm not willing to take the blame for anything, Mitch. No one forced you to have affairs. They're going to vet you big time. How long do you think that make-believe background of yours is going to hold up? Voters don't like it when their politicians lie to them. You lied. You made up a phony background. You pretended to be something you're not. You'll be fodder for the press from now till the election in November. They're going to find out about all those women you had affairs with. Give it up now."

"Oh, I get it. You're right, Julia, sometimes I am stupid. You're having an affair yourself, aren't you? Who is it, one of the pretty doctors you hang out with? One of the guys who speaks your language that I'm too stupid to understand? That's it, isn't it? Well, they'll be vetting you right along with me. How's that going to look to your board of directors? Now, let's get serious here."

Julia poured herself a second cup of coffee. "Yes, let's get serious. I went to the bank yesterday. You've taken three quarters of a million dollars over the years from my account. Where did it go, Mitch? What did you do with it? Like I said, I closed out the account and I'm going to close out the others, too. You can live on your salary and might I also remind you, this is my house, left to me by my father. I can kick your ass out of here any time I want to." She tapped her foot impatiently as she waited for her husband's reply."

"You told me the money was at my disposal. I used it for things. Golf memberships don't come cheap. Clothing isn't cheap. Cars aren't cheap. The cost of dining out is astronomical. I didn't *steal* your money, Julia. You insisted on putting my name on your accounts when we got married. You said what was yours was mine. I believed you. Are you saying you lied to me?"

He was right, she'd done just what he said. But she'd been in love back then and believed her husband loved her. "The well's gone dry. You'll have to live on your salary. I meant it when I said I wanted a divorce."

"Well, I don't want a divorce, and I will fight you. I want this nomination, Julia, and I want you at my side when I accept it."

Julia pretended to think on the matter. Charles would say she overplayed her hand and now she had to backpedal. "I'll tell you what, Mitch. I promise to rethink my feelings but on one condition. I want you to sit down at the table right now and list every single woman you slept with from the day we got married, and the dates and how long the affairs lasted. Just for the record, I am not nor have I ever had an affair. The FBI can vet me from now till the end of time and I will come out clean. Unlike you, I honored my marriage vows. Take it or leave it, you son of a bitch!"

"You want me to do what?" Mitch snarled.

"You heard me the first time." Julia whirled around and fished in one of the kitchen drawers for a pencil and a pad of paper. She tossed them on the table. "Get busy because I have to leave shortly. No list, no marriage."

"You miserable bitch!"

Something snapped in Julia. Her eyes narrowed to slits, venom dripping from her tongue as she let loose. "Listen to me, you bloodsucking son of a bitch, you make the list or I will contact that guy who comes on the FOX network at eight o'clock every night and tell him my story, and your story, and I won't leave a single thing out about our perfect marriage. I'll even tell him about your made up background and that girl Janet Bradshaw the police thought you killed way back when. So you see, you aren't as smart as you think you are. I found out and so will the FBI. Now, goddamn it, write!

"I'm going upstairs to pack. When I get back here, that list better be finished."

In the whole of his life Mitch Webster had never seen such hatred spew from anyone's eyes. He reached for the pencil with the dull point. He started to write. He needed to have the last word, though. "You're going to regret this, bitch!"

"What I regret is the day I married you."

Halfway up the stairs, Julia grasped the railing and sat down on the steps to calm herself. Who was that person back in the kitchen? Her eyes welled up. That was the real Julia Webster, the Julia Webster who could be dying. That's who the person was back in the kitchen.

When she felt strong enough, Julia got to her feet, her legs shaky. She made it the rest of the way up the steps and down the hall to her bedroom. She packed a bag quickly, wondering as she did so if she'd ever come back to this house. If she couldn't go back to the hospital and couldn't come back to this house, where would she go? To the cemetery, next to her father? The tears spilled over and dropped on her hands. She brushed at them impatiently. She still had time.

Julia carried her bag downstairs and set it down by the front door before she made her way to the kitchen. Mitchell was still writing. Julia poured more coffee into the cup she'd left sitting on the counter. She risked a covert glance at the list her husband was writing. Suddenly, she felt sick to her stomach. She had no idea the list would be so long. It would take her forever to weed through the names to find out which of the women had infected her husband with the AIDS virus. She couldn't help but wonder how many of the names on the list she would recognize, how many she knew personally and how many she'd operated on.

"One has to wonder how you had time to perform your senatorial duties, Mitch. That's starting to look like a very impressive list. Did I tell you I want addresses, too?"

"No, you didn't tell me that and no, I am not writing that down because I don't know. I always met them someplace. If your next question is did I ever bring them here, the answer is no."

Julia snatched the list and read through the names. She gasped. "You did . . . and her husband never found out! I guess you were discreet because you'd be dead if he did find out, Mitch. I'm leaving now," she said as she folded the two sheets of paper and put them in her purse.

"Where are you going? What if I need to get in touch with you? The party is less than a week away. The press is going to want to talk to you. I want an answer, Julia."

"It's none of your business where I'm going. Do I ask you where you're going when you leave the house? Have your people call my people. Isn't that what all you power politicians say to each other? I'll call you when I'm ready to call you."

"Then you aren't going to file for divorce?" There was such relief in Mitch's voice, Julia almost laughed. Squirm, you miserable bastard.

"I didn't say that. I said I would think about it. I'm thinking. When I'm done thinking, I'll let you know. Now, get the hell out of my way. I can't bear to look at you. You disgust me."

Julia was outside when she remembered the green plant. She opened the door and walked back to the kitchen. Mitch had the phone to his ear, shocked to see her. What woman was he bleeding to this time? She ignored him as she picked up the plant and left the kitchen.

Seated in her car, she stared across the driveway at Mitch's bright red, $165,000 Porsche.

Two seats. She'd never even ridden in the car her money had paid for. What a fool she was.

For the next four hours, Julia followed the instructions Charles had laid out for her. She shopped, she filled prescriptions, she had a bite to eat and then she headed for a well-known steak house where she parked her car and got out. A dusty black Suburban pulled right next to her car. Julia blinked when she saw Kathryn behind the wheel. She grabbed her bags and the green plant and hoisted herself into the backseat. Murphy barked a greeting from the front seat.

"How ya doing, Miss Daisy?" Kathryn laughed.

"Just peachy. Were you followed?"

"Not that I could see. Were you?"

"If I was, they're good. I don't think so but that doesn't mean anything, as we both know. God, what are we going to do about that D.A.?"

Kathryn drove the Suburban the way she drove her eighteen-wheeler, with gusto. "I guess that's up to Charles. You don't want to know what I'd do to him if it was left up to me. He grilled me months ago when he thought he had the goods on us. The guy is relentless but Nikki had it covered. She's in a bad place, Julia. She still loves the guy but her duty is to the Sisterhood. Hey, how'd it go with the senator?"

Julia told her. "The worst part was, some of those women were friends of mine. There were some I even operated on. I must be naive.

Kathryn, I had no idea there were so many unhappy married women who slept around. I'm thinking he picked married women knowing they wouldn't put the squeeze on him. Married women were safe."

Kathryn leaned on the horn to speed up a gray Taurus that was going too slow for her comfort. When she sailed past him she offered up her middle finger. Julia laughed and didn't know why.

"I know this is a stupid question but are you OK, Julia? What's with the green plant?"

"Yeah, I'm OK. My last checkup was better than I expected. I'm holding my own. The new drugs are terrific. I have some time yet, Kathryn. You don't know how badly I wanted to kill my husband a few hours ago. It was all I could do not to blurt it out. But, like a good little soldier, I held my tongue just the way Charles told me to. I have to find a way to let all those women Mitch had affairs with know they need to get tested but I want to do it anonymously. Charles can help me locate them. I'm having a hard time dealing with the fact that some of my friends slept with my husband and then went to lunch with me the next day."

"Yeah, I'd say that pretty much sucks. My God, Julia, why didn't you ever tell your husband?"

Julia stared out the window. "I had to get used

to . . . to . . . I just had to deal with it first. In the beginning I had to check on every patient I'd operated on in the last year. That took some time. Once I was certain I didn't get infected from one of my patients, I knew it had to be Mitch. I made myself sick over it for a while. I was almost ready to confront him when I met up with Nikki a year or so ago. The rest is history.

"The plant was in my office. No one watered it, and it was dying but I found some plant food in the nurses' kitchen and doctored it up. I guess I felt it was like me, on its last legs. Maybe with some tender loving care, it will come back to life. It has five leaves on it, Kathryn, and one that might or might not fall off. I don't want it to die, that's the bottom line. I thought maybe Myra would let me keep it on the kitchen windowsill for the morning sun."

Kathryn listened to Julia's desperate-sounding voice. "I don't think that's a problem at all. Myra loves green plants."

"But I want to take care of it."

"I don't think that will be a problem either, Julia."

"Good. What did you all do today?"

"We all watched Charles bustle about. He did take a short nap and he was right back at it. We're to meet in the war room after dinner, which, by the way, is a full-blown turkey dinner, just like at Thanksgiving. Baked Alaska for dessert. Murphy is drooling already. For some reason I don't think you're supposed to give a dog turkey. I think I read that somewhere."

"I'm sure Myra will have something for Murphy."

"The dogs are there, Julia. The handler came by this morning and Myra and he talked for a long time. Isabelle is having a dog compound constructed for them for daytime use. They eat red meat. Murphy's nose is out of joint."

"Kathryn, are you worried about Jack Emery?"

"Yeah. So are the others. If we allow him to home in on us, we're going to do a nice long stretch in the federal slammer. Your husband is a goddamn senator."

Murphy started to bark.

Kathryn laughed. "This dog is starting to think of Pinewood as home. We're almost there, Julia. You look tired. No one will mind if you take a nap before dinner."

The gates swung open. Kathryn drove through and then waited a few seconds to make sure they closed behind her before she drove on.

Home sweet home.

"That dinner was scrumptious," Isabelle said as she pushed her chair back from the table. "I feel like going to sleep right now."

Charles stood up and winked at the women.

"That, dear lady, is not an option. I cooked, you all clean up. Trust me, you will wake up rather quickly when you start to scour the pans. I'm off now. Join me when your kitchen duties are finished."

"That baked Alaska will stay on my hips for months," Nikki protested as she, too, started to help clear the table. She looked over at Julia who was staring at the green plant on the kitchen windowsill.

"It should have perked up by now," Julia muttered.

"By tomorrow it will be fine," Myra soothed. Kathryn had clued her in earlier about the plant. "Maybe the plant food was old. It may require repotting. Let's just wait till morning to see how it does, Julia. I've always found philodendrons to be extremely hardy."

"I thought I was hardy, too, and looked what's happening to me," Julia muttered a second time. "I'll scour the pans, you dry, Nikki. We have way too many dishes for the dishwasher as it is."

"No problem," Nikki said, reaching for a dish towel. "I'm not going to be joining you all in the war room. I'm going out to the woods to talk to Jack."

Myra's hand flew to her heart. "Dear, that definitely is not a good idea. Did you tell Charles?"

"Yes, I did tell Charles, Myra. I thought I'd take Murphy with me. He'll pick up Jack's scent and lead me right to him. I worked with Charles all afternoon so I know what's going on. I don't need to be there this evening."

"What if Jack isn't out there tonight? Then what?" Myra asked, her brow furrowed in worry. "And if he is, what are you going to say to him? What if he won't listen? We all deserve to know what you're planning."

"If I knew, Myra, I would tell you. I'm going to wing it. Jack's a wild card and I don't know how he'll react or what he'll do. He is on your property, Myra, and the property is posted, which means he's trespassing. He wouldn't give a little thing like a no trespassing sign a second thought. You can have him arrested because he's breaking the law. In fact, Myra, I want you to give me fifteen minutes and then I want you to call the local police. Murphy and I will guard him and send up a flare. I'd like to see him explain all of this to his superiors."

"But won't that . . . you know . . . *piss* him off even more?"

Nikki threw her arms around Myra. "I love you, Myra," she gurgled. "Yep, it's gonna piss him off big time. But he won't try it a second time. Not if he wants to keep his job. Use your clout, Myra."

Myra looked doubtful. "All right, dear, if you say so." She looked down at her watch. "Should we synchronize our watches?"

Nikki grinned. "Yep, that's a good idea, too.

She looked at both her own and Myra's watch. We're within a minute of each other. Fifteen minutes. No, better make that twenty."

Myra's heart thumped in her chest as she watched Nikki run across the yard and out the gate, Murphy on her heels.

Julia, still busy at the sink, thought about the bag of drugs she'd brought with her at Charles's instructions. Sodium Pentothal had been on the list. She looked down at the last pot in the sink, and shrugged as she reached for a Brillo pad. This was no time for any of them to get squeamish.

Charles eyed the women as they took their seats at the table. From his perch, high above them, he clicked the remote in his hand and Lady Justice appeared on the monitor. She was quickly replaced with a picture of three people staring into the camera.

Charles's voice was cold when he said, "Ladies, meet the Monarch family. The woman on the right is Elaine Monarch. The man on the left is her husband Derek Monarch and the young man in the middle is their son Ethan Monarch. I've compiled a dossier on all three of them and it's in front of you, but for now I want you to pay attention to the background I'm sharing with you. Elaine Monarch is the president of Monarch HMO. Derek is the vice president and Ethan is the secretary treasurer. They've been dickering with the idea of taking the company public but that hasn't happened nor do I see it happening because they want total control.

"Elaine . . ."

"Oh, my God, I gave that woman a face lift," Julia said, interrupting Charles.

Charles didn't miss a beat. He continued right on. "Yes, I know. She inherited a rather large sum of money fifteen years ago and that was used to set up these three HMOs. The stats are in your folder and you can peruse them later. Money flows into Monarch like a raging river and the family spends it at the speed of light. Fortunately, even with all their outrageous spending, they can't spend it all. The company is more than robust. There's over a billion of unspent money that is earning healthy interest every single day. But there is one thing that eludes the Monarchs. They want an Ambassadorship to some country. They don't care if the country is one no one has ever heard of. They'll do anything for that little prize. Just keep it in mind, ladies.

"Mrs. Monarch is a collector. Of everything. At the moment she's into the Ming Dynasty. She's paid out millions for her treasures. Two years ago she was into Japanese collectibles. I understand she has a real Samurai sword and several real robes. Again, she paid out millions for these things.

"The family has houses all over the world. They spend more time in Manassas than any other place because Elaine likes to be near the power brokers in Washington. It's that old ambassador devil she covets. Ideally, they'd like His and Hers ambassadorships. Mrs. Monarch hasn't quite been able to join that elite circle of women who are the real social power brokers. The family is more or less on the fringe, rather like a small band of groupies. They would do anything to land on the A List. It won't happen because just the word HMO leaves a bad taste in everyone's mouth. The politicians accept their money, though, so that puts them way down on the B List. I have it on good authority the family will be at the fund-raising party next week. We have to make that work to our advantage."

"That means all four of our subjects will be under the same roof. Are we going to do a snatch and grab?" Alexis asked.

Charles smiled. "That's exactly what it means. Play close attention. Yoko and Kathryn will be delivering the plants and flowers to the armory. At the end of the evening the plants and flowers will again be loaded into Kathryn's truck and taken to different hospitals and nursing homes in the area.

"Myra, one of this administration's heaviest contributors and right up there at the top of the A List will mingle and approach the Monarch family. She'll stay glued to them, right up to the end when she'll complain about how stuffy it is inside and suggest a breath of fresh air and invite them to join her.

"Julia will be there with her husband, smiling, and doing everything she's supposed to do as the wife of the soon-to-be vice president. Beforehand she will tell him that they both need to get away, to try to patch up their marriage. The plan, as far as Mitchell Webster knows, is they will leave the following morning on Myra's Gulfstream. Their destination, the Caribbean."

Kathryn whooped her pleasure. "Charles, this is so perfect. Where are we taking them? What about Jack Emery?"

Charles held up both hands for silence. "One thing at a time. I haven't definitely decided on where Operation Revenge will take place. Possibly the Monarch home in Manassas, possibly here at Pinewood. I have a great many details to work out first.

"I'm not worried about the senator and Julia. The senator will do whatever Julia wants at this point in time. Before I can plan further, all of you have to tell me what your plan is for the senator and the Monarch family. What's your decision?" He didn't pause long enough for them to answer.

"Now, I know you're all worried about Assistant District Attorney Jack Emery. Myra has a call in to the governor as we speak. For those of you who don't know this, Myra and the governor arc . . . I believe the correct term would be *tight*. The governor will take care of ADA Emery. I don't think I need to spell that out, do I? Of course not, you're all way ahead of me.

"Myra, it's time for you to make your call to the police. You have two minutes. It might be wise for you to stay in the kitchen until the police arrive." Myra nodded. A moment later the secret door to the main house moved and then she was gone.

"We're missing all the fun," Kathryn groused. "I'd pay to see that ADA's ass hauled off to jail."

Yoko tilted her head to the side. "No, you wouldn't, Kathryn, because then you would have to see Nikki's tears and know her heart is breaking. It's better that none of us see that."

Kathryn reached over and squeezed Yoko's slim hand. "You're right, of course. Sometimes I speak before I think."

"Sometimes?" the others squealed. "Sometimes?"

"OK, OK, my mouth is my downfall. Can we move on here?"

"Gladly," Charles said. "Eyes on the monitor please. What I'm going to show you first is some of the decadence of the Monarch family. Then I'm going to show you some still photographs of some of Monarch's subscribers and their families. When I'm finished, I think you'll find it quite easy to come up with a suitable punishment for the Monarch family."

Charles stepped down to the main floor and walked over to Julia's chair. "When I'm finished with the stills of the Monarch family I plan to show photos of the women your husband had affairs with. It's not very pretty, Julia, so if you want to join Myra in the kitchen, it will be fine with all of us. It's up to you."

Julia clenched her teeth so hard she thought her jaw would crack. Her voice was firm, however, when she said, "I'll stay, Charles. It's not like I haven't known about them."

"All right, ladies, here we go!"

Nikki, Murphy at her side, entered the piney forest where she'd played as a child with Myra's daughter Barbara. She knew every inch of the vast forest. Oh, how they'd run and scampered out here. One time they'd even pitched a tent. Scared out of their wits, they'd managed to make it through the night with sugar cookies and peanut butter and jelly sandwiches. It wasn't until later that they found out Myra had been less than a hundred yards away making sure they were safe. They'd ridden their ponies through the forest and had picnics almost every day during the summers they were home from school.

A lump formed in her throat at her memories. Barbara was gone now and Nikki missed her terribly.

How fragrant the forest was. She sniffed ap-

preciativcly. "Oh, Jack! Come out wherever you
are! C'mon, Jack, don't make me search all
night! I know you're up there in one of those
trees spying on Myra and everyone in the house.
Be a man and come down out of that tree!
Don't make me come up there after you!" Nikki
shouted. When there was no response, Nikki
looked down at Murphy. "Go get him, Murph!"
The huge shepherd raced off, Nikki right on his
heels.

When Murphy skidded to a halt and started
to growl, Nikki slowed down. She casually meandered over to a tree and flashed the beam of her
flashlight upward. "It's supposed to rain tonight,
Jack! Come on down and let's go into the house
for some coffee. It's going to be a very cold spring
rain. You know you're trespassing, right?"

Jack Emery cursed as he slid down the tree.
"The stars are out so I doubt it's going to rain.
The temperature is seventy. Trespassing? I didn't
damage the tree. I was communing with nature.
Isn't that what you're doing, Counselor? So, run
me off. Or are you planning on calling the cops?
Nice doggie," Jack said, attempting to pat Murphy
on the head. The shepherd growled once, then
again, before he lunged. Nikki pulled him back
before his teeth could sink into Jack's arm.

Nikki's laugh sounded forced to her ears.
"Do I look like I'm calling the cops? Go ahead,
search me, I don't even have my cell phone with
me. I came out here to tell you to get off Myra's

property. She doesn't like it when people spy on her. You were spying on her, Jack. And guess what else, I don't like it either. You're really becoming a pain in my ass, ADA Emery."

"Then fess up and I'll get out of your hair," Jack said coldly.

"That ain't gonna happen, Jack, since only a fool would confess to something they didn't do. Get over that cockamamie notion you have that Myra did something illegal. I don't want to hear your theory that rich people are above the law."

"You're pretty cocky there, Counselor. Does it have anything to do with Myra's house guest, the one whose hubby's going to be the next veep? Poor choice. The guy's a dud."

"Be that as it may, it's none of your business who Myra entertains."

"Sure it is, Nik. That just shoots old Myra right up there on the Washington power pole."

"You're paranoid where Myra is concerned. You need to get over Marie Llewellyn. So you had her under house arrest. So she took off on you. She had help. It was a wild and stormy night. Stop blaming yourself and stop trying to pin her disappearance on Myra. In other words, get over it, Jack."

"Then why did you dump me? We were engaged, Nik. We were supposed to get married. You said you'd love me forever. When push came to shove, you chose Myra over me. There had to be a pretty strong reason for you to do something like that."

"Yeah. Like maybe Myra adopting me when my parents died? Like maybe Myra taking care of me, sending me to college and being a mother to me. Yeah, I'd say that's a pretty damn strong reason to side with her. It didn't have to be that way but you're so damn pig-headed you wouldn't listen to reason."

Jack pushed his billed camouflage cap farther back on his head. He was so damn weary. "You're blowing smoke, trying to divert me. It's not going to work, Nik."

Oh, isn't it? Nikki thought as she saw pinpoints of light in the distance. Her stomach started to crunch up at the thought of the police taking Jack off in handcuffs. Jack saw the lights at the same time and prepared to run, but Murphy had other ideas.

"Stop where you are and put your hands in the air," came the command. Nikki's hands shot in the air in the blink of an eye. Jack wasn't quite as fast but his hands did go up.

"You witch! You miserable, lying witch! You called the cops and tricked me! Jesus, what the hell *are* you women doing in that house? This is a new low even for you, Nik."

Nikki didn't respond, she was too choked up. She started off in the direction of the house. She knew if she looked back, she'd crumble into a million pieces. She started to run but Murphy beat her by a nose. She collapsed in Myra's arms.

"Are you all right, dear?"

Not "What happened, is he going to turn us in?" No, that wasn't Myra. Myra loved her and her first concern was her welfare. Whatever Jack did or said, she would deal with.

"I'm OK, Myra. They took him off in handcuffs. I didn't stick around to watch but I did hear the clink of the cuffs. He was madder than a wet rooster, I can tell you that. There was a little name-calling but nothing I can't handle. Myra, he isn't going to give up. We have to make some decisions."

Myra wrapped Nikki in her arms. "I've taken care of everything, dear. I called the governor. Word will filter down to the right people within the hour. Mr. Emery will not be bothering us any longer."

Nikki gasped. "You called the governor of Virginia because . . . because . . ."

"Because ADA Emery is becoming a thorn in our side. As you know, Tyson Jackson is a personal friend. He's been here to dinner more times than I can remember and I am the godmother of his first grandchild. One always calls upon one's friends when one is in trouble, although I didn't say I was in trouble. Tyson said he would take care of the matter, so we don't have to worry about Mr. Emery any longer. I took care of everything, dear, so don't worry."

Nikki slapped at her forehead. "Oh, God, Myra, that's where you're wrong. You don't know Jack. Having the governor intervening on your behalf will just convince him that we're up to something. I want you to believe me when I tell you Jack will quit his job and make this personal. He's like that, a dog with a bone. He never gives up until he gets a conviction. What we did tonight was piss him off to the nth degree. Now, he'll be out for blood. This is all my fault, Myra. I shouldn't have had you call the cops. I wish you had told me you were going to call the governor."

"Maybe I wasn't cut out for this spy game," Myra said as she led Nikki and Murphy into the house. "It's starting to rain, dear. We should roll up the awning on the terrace. Never mind, let it get wet, who cares?"

"Jack didn't believe me when I told him it was going to rain," Nikki said.

Myra whirled around. "Is that important, Nicole?"

In spite of herself, Nikki burst out laughing. "No, Myra, it isn't important. The damn awning isn't important either. Neither is Jack getting arrested."

"Would you like some hot cocoa, dear?"

"God, no, Myra. I'm going to bed."

"Good night, dear. Sleep tight," Myra said as she pecked Nikki on the cheek.

"You, too, Myra."

* * *

A hollow-eyed, unshaven Jack Emery marched into his office. No one looked at him. Maybe he smelled. He was angrier than he'd ever been in his life. One night in jail could do that to a person. He'd been released on his own recognizance and told to report to his superior, Chad Bartlett, stat, which meant immediately in D.A. speak. So, here he was. And there was District Attorney Chad Bartlett, clean-shaven, dewy-eyed and smelling like the prairie.

"Don't say a word, Emery, not one goddamn word. I got a call from the police commissioner last night. He actually woke me up. He said he got a call from the mayor. It seems the mayor got a call from the governor. You following me here, Jack?"

Jack winced. "Yes, sir."

"It seems that Ms. Myra Rutledge called her good friend Tyson Jackson over at the governor's mansion and said you were perched in a tree and trespassing and spying on her and her guests and she wanted you arrested and she didn't want it to happen again. And then this morning, my secretary handed me a copy of this police report that has your name on it. You better have a damn good explanation, son."

Jack licked at his dry lips. The inside of his mouth felt and smelled like his old sneakers. He cleared his throat. "I believe Myra Rutledge and a group of her friends are involved in illegal activities. I think they're the ones who spirited Marie Llewellyn . . ."

"Stop right there, Emery. The woman disappeared on your watch. You take responsibility for that. We've been over that, up and down that, and we even went over it crossways. Myra Rutledge had a rock solid alibi on that night. Don't go there again, Emery. This has something to do with your fiancée, according to your coworkers. If I even get a sniff of something going on where you and your colleagues are concerned, I'll personally throw the book at you. Miss Rutledge, her friends and her adopted daughter Nicole Quinn will be forever off-limits to you. All I need is one sniff, Jack, that you aren't following orders, and it's all over."

Jack's mind raced as he tried to calculate how much money he had in his account. Maybe he could draw on his 401K. "I need to apply for a thirty-day leave of absence, sir," he said stiffly.

"Denied. Is there anything else?"

"Sir, my mother is ill. She's in a nursing home. I need the time. If you can't see to granting the leave then I have to resign." His mother was ill and in a nursing home but his taking a month off wouldn't help her in any way. It could all be verified. *Liar, liar, pants on fire.* Whatever it takes, Emery, whatever it takes.

"All right, Jack, I'll give you the month with the understanding and the promise that you will not harass or cause Myra Rutledge one iota of trouble. Assign your pending cases to whomever you think is best equipped to handle them. Remember what I said, one sniff of anything improper and your ass is on the unemployment line."

"Yes, sir. Thank you, sir."

"Go home and take a bath, for God's sake. You're smelling up my office. And, Emery, Ms. Rutledge, fine woman that she is, will not press charges if you toe the line. Step over it and you're in the slammer. Go on, get out of here!"

An hour later, Jack Emery was back in his apartment, hunched over his computer. The small television he kept on the kitchen counter was turned on to CNN, his favorite news channel. He felt lower than a snake's belly as he mapped out his itinerary for the next thirty days. He'd used up all his favors with his friends so he was on his own. He knew in his gut if he made one misstep, his ass would go in a sling and he'd be out of a job. If he wasn't careful, he could be living on the street.

The headache pounding inside his skull was louder than a bongo drum. Where the hell should he start? With those women of course. He hadn't been lying to Nikki when he said he'd run profiles on every one of them. They were as complete as Lexis Nexis could make them. He turned when he heard the name Webster on the television. The doctor's husband, Senator Webster, was going to be Governor Crawford's running mate in the presidential election. Whoa!

Jack sat back in his swivel chair, his mind racing. If it was true, and CNN rarely got it wrong, why was Dr. Webster hanging out at Pinewood? Shouldn't she be at her husband's side, being interviewed over and over again? He put a large red question mark on Julia's folder. Then he added a second one for emphasis. She'd consulted Nikki Quinn's law firm but whatever went down there was considered privileged.

He moved on to Isabelle Flanders. He studied the report. At the height of her career she'd been involved in a terrible car accident killing an entire family. He remembered the case well. Her defense had been beyond weak, blaming her assistant for the accident. Till the end of the trial she'd professed her innocence. She'd lost everything, her home, her business, her reputation. She'd floundered for a while, working in a dress shop, a convenience store and other menial jobs. She'd consulted with Nikki's firm but again it was privileged.

Alexis Thorne wasn't really Alexis Thorne at all. She'd been convicted of securities fraud and sent to prison. She'd served her time, gotten out, and changed her name, presumably with Nikki's help since she, too, had consulted with Nikki's legal firm. Now she worked as a personal shopper to the rich and famous. Again, everything was privileged.

Kathryn Lucas. He flinched when he remembered how he'd had her and her eighteen-wheeler hauled into the compound. He'd grilled her, with Nikki representing her, but he'd gotten nothing from the woman. Dead husband. She worked with a ferocious dog, the same dog who'd held him at bay last night in the woods. He had no clue as to why a truck driver would consult Nikki's high-end law firm.

Yoko Akia had consulted Nikki, too, possibly for incorporation of her garden nursery. Nothing out of the ordinary had surfaced on his various searches for her or her husband. For all intents and purposes, both husband and wife were who and what they said they were.

Jack chewed on his lower lip. The one thing they all had in common was Nikki. There was no way that group of women would have found Myra Rutledge on their own. None of them had anything in common with Myra. It all came back to Nikki.

Jack got up to take some aspirin and to make coffee. One of these days, he thought, I really have to get some sleep. I can't keep going on pure adrenaline. He stared out his kitchen window as he tried to make sense of everything.

Nikki knew all the women, probably represented them all or, at the very least, counseled them. Myra had the money. Maybe she was helping the women on Nikki's advice. Myra was known for her philanthropy. But this time she was all over the map. Odd for Myra.

One thing he was certain of, the women didn't meet up at Pinewood to play cards. They met up to . . . to . . . do what? Jack had to admit he didn't have a clue. Then there was the business with the pack of Dobermans. Myra never felt the need to have guard dogs in the past. Why now all of a sudden? Why was everyone so bent out of shape because he was spying on them? What were they afraid he would see? He wrote the word SECRET in big red letters on top of Nikki's folder. All he had to do was find out what the secret was.

Jack slouched up against the kitchen counter while he waited for the coffee to finish dripping into the pot. He'd purposely made the coffee strong, so strong it looked like tar. For sure his eyeballs would pop to attention.

The secret! What the hell was the secret? Think, Emery. How in the hell was he going to find out what it was since Nikki chopped him off at the knees?

Jack carried his coffee back to his desk, shifted his mental gears to what he called his neutral zone, and let his mind take off. Everything went haywire with Nikki when Myra's daughter was killed. Good, good, Emery, great jumping-off spot. Nikki changed then and so did their relationship. Then came Marie Llewellyn's trial.

He'd prosecuted her because that was his job. It didn't mean he didn't feel the woman's pain. He wasn't heartless. *Hell, if someone raped my daughter who knows what I would do. I was doing my goddamn job was what I was doing.* He scribbled furiously. The rape killer had gotten off scot-free thanks to a creative defense team. Then when the killer walked down the court steps, Marie Llewellyn pulled out a gun and shot him. Right in front of the whole world to see on their television sets.

Llewellyn had been arrested. Nik got pissed off. Myra posted a million dollars bail to get the woman placed under house arrest. There had been a rumor going around that Myra had called her old friend the governor to intercede on the bail, a rumor that Nik refused to confirm or deny. Nik asked him not to prosecute because she was going to defend Llewellyn. He'd refused. They had one fight after the other. Nik sided with Myra. Oh yeah, Nik sided with Myra. Myra again. Filthy rich Myra. Jack continued to scribble.

Ooops. Back up, Emery. According to Nik, Myra was the next thing to catatonic over the death of her daughter. Then, all of a sudden, Myra is full of piss and vinegar and wants Nik to defend Marie Llewellyn. Myra posts the outrageous bail. What's wrong with this picture, he wondered. He scribbled some more.

Then just before trial, Marie Llewellyn and

her family disappear. For all intents and purposes, they simply walked out of the house, leaving everything behind. On one of the stormiest nights of the year. The children's toys, their bank books, food, their cars—everything was left behind. They weren't rich. In fact their savings account held a meager $751. Their checking account held $81.25. The family walked away with whatever they had in their pockets.

Because . . . because . . . They had help. He'd gone so far as to accuse Nik and Myra of spiriting the family away. Of course they'd denied any and all involvement. That's when things had really soured between himself and Nik.

Myra had flourished, though, while Nik just got more hateful. Then Nik moved back to the farm and the card games started. "Card games my ass," Jack muttered.

Jack spent the next ten minutes taping together sheets of paper that he then taped to his living room wall. With a red marker he proceeded to draw a map, enter notes and draw arrows all over the place. He mumbled as he swirled and twirled his marker until he was satisfied. He stared at the names on the right hand side of his map. Okayyyyy. The red marker scrawled across the page. More arrows followed.

Nikki and Myra. Myra and Nikki. The brains and the money. The money and the brains. What the hell were they into? Something serious, that's for sure. But what?

119

The red marker moved again. Doctor, florist, architect, securities broker turned personal shopper, truck driver, lawyer, rich woman. Then there was Charles. Just who the hell was he?

Truck. Medicine. Architect. Flowers. Legal. Money. Truck. Jack drew a big red circle around the word truck. An eighteen-wheeler. You could put two cars in one of those babies. Webster was a plastic surgeon. Maybe she gave the Llewellyn family a whole new look. How far-fetched was *that*? The red marker moved again and again. The truck could have been used to spirit the family away. Now *that* was not far-fetched.

Myra's money could have been used to give the family a new identity. Not far-fetched at all. Nikki was part of it. The brains.

But . . . That was all months and months ago. Why were the women still meeting at Pinewood? The same women. Why did Nikki take a leave of absence from her job and her teaching position?

It was a club. A goddamn fucking club of some kind where those seven women did . . . what did they do? Something outside the law? Something they needed Nikki to orchestrate while Myra paid the bills.

Jack went back to the kitchen to pour more coffee into his cup. It was still hot, still black, and it tasted like crap. He drank it anyway.

He was closing in, getting a handle on things. He could feel it. Nikki used to tease him about his gut instincts while he teased her about her woman's intuition. What a match they were. And now it was all gone.

Maybe he needed some expert help. Someone with clearer vision, someone who could be objective. Maybe his old friend Mark Lane in the J. Edgar Hoover Building. He thought about it for all of ten seconds before he reached for the phone but suddenly, he couldn't remember the number. That had to mean he hadn't called his buddy in a long time. He fumbled for his address book and dialed Mark's cell phone. The FBI agent picked up on the third ring. Jack identified himself and they talked pleasantries until Mark said, "I hope to hell you aren't calling me because you want me to get you some information from the FBI database."

"Nah. I want you to meet me for a drink. I have a story to tell you and I need your analytical input. Yeah, I'm paying. I invited you, didn't I? No, Nikki and I are on the outs. Actually, she dumped me. Yeah, yeah, I couldn't believe it either. She'll never find anyone half as good as me. Yeah, I'm saying that with a straight face. Seven o'clock at Mc Guire's. See ya, buddy."

Jack spent the next few hours going over his finances. If he sold his skis, his snowboard, his snorkeling gear, took cash advances on his credit cards that were almost to the max, plus what he could wrangle out of his 401K, he should be able to get through the month, pay his rent, his car payment, the minimum on his plastic and eat macaroni and cheese, and peanut butter and jelly, he might squeak by. But, just in case, he went online and applied for a new credit card and then filled out the forms to increase his credit line on his existing cards.

His mind going full blast, he headed for the shower. He emerged feeling almost like his old self. It was always this way when he was closing in on the tail end of a case.

With nothing else to occupy his time, Jack went back on the computer to do more searches on the women who played cards at Pinewood.

Two hours later, Jack walked back to the kitchen, this time for a beer. Alexis Thorne's case bothered him. Nothing in her background even alluded to the fact that she was dishonest. On the contrary. She'd protested her innocence, said she was set up, but she was convicted anyway. She was from a poor black family but she'd worked her way through college. She belonged to the drama club because she wanted to be an actress but didn't have the talent, so she'd gone into costume and makeup and learned all the tricks of the trade.

When she graduated from college she'd gone to work in a small brokerage firm where she was able make use of her education while still pursuing her drama hopes by volunteering her services for Little Theater. Her mentor, a guy named Cyril Therman, had bequeathed his "bag of tricks" to Alexis on his death bed. Or so said the only interview Alexis had ever given after being convicted of securities fraud. Some smart-ass lawyer must have told her a good human interest story would go a long way at her sentencing. It hadn't.

Jack went back to his map on the wall and wrote the words makeup, costumes, disguise. It sort of went with Dr. Webster's specialty, plastic surgery. Underneath he wrote the word "innocent" with a large question mark. His heart started to thump in his chest when he moved down to Isabelle Flanders's name. She, too, said she was innocent. Said one of her trusted employees was driving the car that killed a family.

Two women who claimed to be innocent of the crimes they were convicted of.

Well, what have we here? A lot of loose ends. Maybe Mark would see something he wasn't seeing. Maybe.

Seven o'clock couldn't come soon enough for him.

It was like every other bar in D.C. All mahogany, brass, and sawdust on the floor. A local watering hole for the young hipsters and government workers. The only problem was you couldn't hear yourself think, much less carry on a conversation. However, it was a good place to ogle the sleek young female lawyers with their tight suits and roving eyes. With no interest in ogling anyone, Jack had chosen seven o'clock to meet up with Mark because the five o'clock crowd was starting to leave and the evening customers hadn't arrived yet. He figured he had a forty-five minute window to tell Mark his story and get his feedback.

Like old buddies, they clapped each other on the back before they bellied up to the mahogany bar for their Buds and waited for a table to clear in the back of the bar. While they waited they dissected every female within eye range, a temporary distraction to pass the time. When a table cleared they beelined to it and yelled their order to a cute waitress who grinned at them. Her skimpy shorts, long legs and tight spandex top did not go unnoticed.

Jack blurted out his story as he played with the long-neck in his hands. When he finally wound down he said, "I need you to tell me if I'm nuts or if I've got something going on here."

Mark removed his glasses, pinched the bridge of his nose and then settled the wire rims more firmly before he spoke. "Man, you got something going on here. You took a fucking month off just to work on this! What if you can't nail it by the end of the month?"

Jack eyed the pudgy man sitting across from him. His dark brown eyes behind his wire rimmed glasses were starting to steam up with his excitement. It looked to Jack like Mark was losing his hair, too. Better not to mention something so personal. Damn, it had been a while since they'd seen each other. "I don't know, Mark. I just know I gotta do it. What's your spin on this?"

"Off the top of my head, and it's a wild guess on my part, I think you're looking at a bunch of female vigilantes. What's with that Charles character?"

Jack shrugged.

"Maybe he's the brains of the outfit. Excuse me but I think you're giving Nikki too much credit here and, besides, you want it to be her so you can get even with her. How'm I doing so far?"

"To what end? Who? What? Where?"

"How the hell do I know? You just told me the damn story. The only player I know is Nikki. Maybe that Llewellyn babe was their first shot. Hey, it worked, smart ass. She's gone and it was on your watch. Maybe they're gearing up for something else. The only thing of interest going on in this town right now is Senator Webster being picked to be Crawford's running mate. Both parties are sniping at each other. Nothing new there. No big time stuff out of the ordinary is going on at the Bureau. The world is a crazy place these days, Jack."

Their double burgers and sides of fries arrived along with two more long-necks. The friends wolfed down the burgers and ordered seconds.

While they waited, Jack said, "What would you do if you were me?"

"Go home and get under the covers and don't come out till the end of the month. How the hell should I know what you should do? You're not going to leave it alone, are you?"

Jack shook his head.

"That's what I thought." Mark sighed. "OK, what do you want me to do?"

"You're pretty much a nine-to-five guy. Help me out at night. See what you can come up with on Charles Martin and Senator Webster. In the morning I'll drop off the files I've accumulated unless you want to go home with me and get them tonight. By the way, how's your love life?"

"In the dumps like yours. Don't go there, Jack. You're gonna owe me for this."

"Yeah, I know. Good burgers, eh?" Jack said, chomping down on his.

Between mouthfuls of food, Mark asked, "Just how rich is Myra Rutledge?"

"Fortune 500 company. Did I say she's personal friends of the governor? She called him last night to get me off the property. Don't you think that's a stretch?"

Mark belched, then apologized. "Depends on what she's involved in and what she's trying to hide. Everyone needs a big gun to call on when their ass is about to be nailed to the wall. It doesn't get any better than being on a first name basis with the governor of this fine state."

Jack leaned back in his chair. "You're my big gun, Mark."

"God help us both, Jack, if I'm the best you can do."

Six

"Are you ready, girls?" Myra all but squealed, her face alight with excitement.

"We're ready, we're ready. Show us! Myra, stop torturing us," Isabelle shouted to be heard over the din of the others.

"All right, all right! Our outfits arrived just minutes ago. I couldn't wait to show them to you and Charles is slightly miffed that I pulled you all out of the command center. Fashions first! Who wants to go first?"

"Me! Please let it be me," Yoko said.

Myra smiled as she rummaged among the tissue paper in the huge white box that had arrived by courier. She withdrew an electric blue

gown with a stand up collar and a generous slit
that was thigh high. The gown was so severe it
shrieked dollar signs. Yoko rolled her eyes in ec-
stasy. "I've never had anything so grand. Thank
you, Myra."

"Kiddo, you are going to look like the em-
press of China. Was she beautiful?"

Yoko giggled. "No, but that is all right. I will
accept the compliment."

Myra rummaged again among the tissue paper.
"This is for you, Julia," she said, handing over a
slim, gold leaf dress with a high neck and long
sleeves.

"Oh, this is too gorgeous for words," Julia
said. "I love the way the dress flares at the ankle.
Matching shoes. I hope I don't have to do much
walking."

"Not to worry, dear. We'll take your rubber
soled shoes in the limousine when we have to . . .
ah . . . burn rubber." She held out a scarlet dress
to Kathryn who blinked.

"I'm going to feel naked, Myra. I never wore a
strapless gown in my life. Are you sure it will stay
up?"

Alexis giggled. "I'll make sure it stays up. It's
gorgeous. Absolutely gorgeous."

Nikki's gown was black shot through with silver threads. Isabelle ooohed and aaahed over
her white crepe gown with spaghetti straps and
a flare at the knees. Alexis reached for her gown
that was the color of sienna. It too was strapless.

"Show us yours, Myra. What color did you choose?" the women asked all at the same time.

"I chose dusty rose and my gown has a hip length sheer coat. Silver shoes and bag. I'm so glad you all like your dresses. It was so hard to choose."

"Who is the designer?" Kathryn asked, peering at the label.

"No one famous. Yet. I expect she will be after Saturday night, though. Be sure to tell the press your outfits were designed by Callie. That's the name she goes by. Her real name is Calista Cole. She's a client of Nikki's. I think we should be getting back to Charles. We certainly don't want him upset today of all days."

"No, we certainly don't want to do that because then he'll serve us wieners for dinner. I hate wieners. Isn't today the day . . . ?"

"The day Charles drops the first bombshell to the tabloids on Mitch. Yep," Julia said happily as she led the way down the steps and across the hall to the living room where Myra opened the secret door to what she called Charles's Lair.

The women filed into the war room and took their seats. Their thoughts, however, were back in Myra's bedroom with the Callie fashions they would all be wearing in a little over thirty-six hours. They came back to reality when Charles homed in on Julia. He didn't say anything but waited for her to speak, his eyes full of questions.

131

"I haven't actually spoken to Mitch, Charles. He's called numerous times and left messages. The last message he left said he is the definite choice although he and the governor are the only ones who know that. The official announcement and his acceptance will be made on Saturday evening. They always pretend no one knows but everyone inside the Beltway knows before it even happens. Some of his messages weren't too nice but then Mitch isn't very nice these days. I did leave one message saying I would be home this evening. I really don't want to go until tomorrow. The less time I have to spend with him, the better."

"Tomorrow will be fine, Julia. I don't want you to put any undue stress on yourself. Our first little tidbit will hit the airwaves around noon today. I already sent an anonymous E-mail to one of the tabloids. It goes without saying that the senator will be unavailable for comment. He'll call the charge scurrilous and say it was put out by the other side. A dirty tricks campaign. By next week it will be a free-for-all. Now, have you all come up with a plan of action?"

"We have, Charles, but we need to know the location before we can put it into play."

Charles pressed a button on his remote. A blueprint sprang into view. Charles clicked the remote again to enlarge the print on the screen. "This is the floor plan of the Monarch house in Manassas. I considered several choices but in the end this one won out. Because, just in case anyone sees the truck or the limo entering the estate, it will be OK. Everyone got invited back to the Monarch home for drinks after the party. There's nothing unusual about that at all.

"I've taken the liberty of arranging vacations for the help. All six of them, a housekeeper, cook, chauffeur, gardener and two maids will board Myra's Gulfstream for a fully paid three week vacation in the Caribbean. The Monarchs have always been more than generous with their servants so this will not raise any eyebrows. They will board the plane right after the Monarchs leave for the party, having been told by the new chauffeur that their employers are going to Europe for a month.

"I've engaged the services of several operatives whom I trust implicitly. They will open the house, clear the alarm system, deactivate the security gates outside and then put us in a lockdown mode until our mission is completed. Are there any questions?"

There was only one question, posed by Yoko. "What about Jack Emery?"

Nikki was about to reassure her when Charles quietly responded to the question. "ADA Emery has taken a thirty day leave of absence. He is under surveillance and will remain under surveillance for the next thirty days. If he goes anywhere near any of you, we'll know in an instant and in that instant we will be forced to make a decision. Do you all understand what I just said?"

Nikki looked everywhere but at Charles.

"Would you care to divulge your plans for the senator and the Monarchs?" Charles asked as though he was inquiring about the weather.

"Actually, Charles, we're winging this one. We want you and Myra to come back here after the party. That means you'll have to engage two limousines for Saturday night. I'll dismiss the driver who takes Mitch and myself by saying we're going with friends for drinks. No details."

"That's not a problem. You'll all have your secure cell phones and we will be available should you need us."

"Charles, would you mind bringing up that blueprint again and printing it out for us. There's a home theater in the house, isn't there?"

"Complete with popcorn machine. And a bowling alley and an indoor pool."

"What about computer equipment?" Nikki asked.

"They have it all, Nikki."

"A safe?" Alexis queried.

Charles smiled. "Several, as a matter of fact. One vault. I marked them with big red Xs on the original copy. If your next question is where do they keep their business records, the answer is in the floor safe in the laundry room. The Monarchs cart those records with them everywhere they go."

The women eyed Charles with baffled expressions.

"How do you know this?" Yoko squeaked.

Charles smiled. "Let's just say I know, and leave it at that."

"Which safe holds their personal bank records? I'm assuming you know that, too, right?" Isabelle asked.

Charles chuckled. "Of course I know the answer. The box spring in the guest bedroom on the second floor, the second room going down the hall, has been hollowed out in the center. The records are right there just waiting for you. The Monarchs seldom have guests while they're in Manassas so the maids aren't overly zealous in their cleaning duties."

Kathryn's eyes widened in awe. "And you know this . . . how? Never mind. I'm sorry I asked."

Charles smiled. He loved it when he could surprise the sisters. He reached across to the printer for the copies of the Monarchs' floor plans and passed them around the table. He was back at his computer station in a second. He turned the volume up on one of the television monitors.

The women looked upward and gasped.

"Can this be true?" someone named Jared on the FOX network asked a visiting guest.

The guest, a retired something-or-other, the way most of FOX's guests were, grimaced as he shrugged his shoulders. "I think this is Washington political spin. If you're asking me if Senator Webster is a philanderer, my answer is I have no way of knowing. You could ask him for a comment."

Charles risked a glance at Julia who was biting down on her lower lip, her hands clenched into fists on the table.

"The senator hasn't been available for comment. His aide said it was hogwash and just spin because his boss is on the short list."

A second retired something-or-other spoke up. "Where there's smoke there's fire. I would be interested in the women's comments. I understand one name is already public and up on Matt Drudge's Web site. Hey, we're talking about the veep nomination. The ghouls are out there. Both sides do the same thing. They have specialists who dig up dirt; we all know that."

Jared looked from one to the other of his retired guests. "What do you think something like this will do to his nomination?"

The first retiree spoke up, "Depends whether Webster comes out and makes a comment. It's usually best to be front and center and bite the bullet. If he waffles and the press comes up with proof, he's dead in the water."

The second retiree smirked. "All the senator needs to do is admit to a little dalliance, with his wife on his arm saying she knew and forgave him a long time ago."

Jared looked into the camera and said, "Thank

you, gentlemen, I'm sorry to cut you short but we're heading into a hard break."

Charles turned down the volume on the television. "Any comments?"

Julia looked sick at what she'd just seen. "Mitch won't make a comment. He's too arrogant. He'll call it bullshit smut being dug up by the other side to embarrass him. Or, he might accuse me of leaking it all for my own personal reasons. One thing I know for certain, he will be absolutely livid. Ah, my phone is vibrating." Julia reached to her belt where her cell phone was clipped. "Yes, it's Mitchell. Obviously, I am not going to answer the phone."

"Having said that, I suggest we get down to work, girls," Alexis said. "Charles, are we going to the party under our own names or are we using aliases? Do we have invitations? Do we need to alter our appearance?"

"Yes, to everything. Aliases of course. I created copies of the invitation from Myra's original. And, yes, ladies, you all need to alter your appearance, not that you aren't beautiful as you are. Nothing drastic, slight changes so if anyone is asked to recall any of you, their description at best will be vague. Myra and I will be going as ourselves since we will be returning here after the party. We always go to these functions so we're not going to appear out of place. I'm going to leave you for a while to do whatever you have to do. I'll start dinner. Myra, keep your eye on the oven. Oh, one last thing. Julia, let me know when you leave. I want to make sure you're not followed and I want you kept safe. Promise me."

Julia felt a lump form in her throat. "I promise."

Seven

Mark Lane cursed as he wedged his way into traffic, three cars behind the shiny black Mercedes. He didn't like a three-car lead; two was best if you didn't want to lose the person you were tailing. Since he had Dr. Webster's home address, he wasn't too worried that he might lose her in late Friday night traffic. Still, Jack would pitch a fit if he did lose the woman and she went somewhere else. Where the hell would she go in the pouring rain? Women didn't like to get their hair wet. Nah, she was going home. He called Jack who was somewhere on the same road he was, tailing the big rig with the two women who had left earlier.

Mark reached over to the passenger seat for

his cell phone and worked his speed dial. "Where are you, kemosabe?"

"Sitting in traffic. Where are you?" came the response.

"Tailing the doctor. Do you believe this rain? I'd probably make better time if I got out and started to swim. She's three cars ahead of me. Don't worry, I'm not going to lose her. I have eyes like a hawk. Where's that rig going?"

"Alexandria would be my guess. The Asian girl buys in volume from that particular nursery. Why she's going there at this hour of the night is beyond me. Wouldn't surprise me one bit if she isn't doing the decorating at the armory for the shindig tomorrow. You can fit a lot of plants in back of one of those rigs."

"Listen, Jack, I have to hang up. It's raining harder and we're coming up to a few exits. If I can't see in this glop, I might miss her."

The wipers on Lane's Pathfinder worked furiously against the driving rain. Visibility was almost nil with a low fog starting to roll in. Mark cursed again until he saw the Mercedes inch to the right. Good, she was getting off the highway. He wasn't sure but he thought he left the fog behind. If there was one thing in life he hated, it was fog with a bunch of asshole Washington drivers.

He was behind her now and within minutes knew she was indeed headed to Georgetown. He followed her as far as Dumbarton, parked, got out and ran back to the street where the doctor lived. Mark pulled up the hood of his sweatshirt as he pretended to be on his way home. He passed the senator's driveway aware that the doctor was just sitting in her car with the lights off. What did that mean?

Mark continued walking to the corner, then doubled back. Ah, she was getting out of the car and walking toward the front door. He stepped behind a firethorn bush and tried to ignore the rain dripping down his neck. Looks like the senator is home, too, he thought as he peered through the leaves of the firethorn bush at a spiffy Porsche sitting right next to the Mercedes. These people paid more for their cars than he'd earn in five years, maybe seven. Shit!

He watched as Dr. Webster started toward the house. A sensor light came on and he could see her clearly. She looked tired and unhappy. She also didn't look like she was in a hurry to enter the house. As she drew closer he saw something else he wasn't expecting to see. He saw the doctor raise her hand and bless herself before she entered the house. Son of a bitch!

Mark raced back to where he'd parked his car on Dumbarton. He worked his speed dial a second time. Jack sounded tired when he responded.

"OK, buddy, our bird's in the nest. Listen, I have to tell you something. Our bird is scared out of her wits. I was *this* close to her, behind a bush. Her feet were dragging. She didn't want to go into that house. She also made the sign of the cross before she opened the door. I don't feel right leaving but I'm not supposed to be here. My section chief will string me up by my balls if he finds out. Should I go home now?"

"Yeah, go on home, Mark. I owe you. We're just observing. We can't interfere. For starters, I live in Virginia. Yeah, yeah, you fibbies supercede us dicks. But I don't want you getting your ass in a sling with your boss either. You sure we're covered for tomorrow night? I don't want to show up and get my ass bounced outta there."

"Section chief approved it. We got more than a dozen guys out with some kind of crud. The gig tomorrow night is considered a big shit detail. My boss hates these things and is grateful for your help. I don't know how grateful he'd be if he knew why you wanted to be at the armory tomorrow night. Tobias approved you and signed off on it. I have the papers right here in the car. We're supposed to show up at four-thirty. We're teamed together and working the parking lot. If it rains, we're screwed."

"It's not going to rain, Mark. The rain is supposed to clear out by morning. My girls are doing just what I thought they were doing, loading the truck with plants and flowers. I'm going home now myself. Make sure you're back at Myra's by eight o'clock tomorrow morning."

"Listen, Jack, I don't feel right about leaving. I'm worried about that woman but I guess you're right, we can't get involved." Mark made a right-hand turn and drove through a mini pond. "Jack, did you hear the news today?"

"Is somebody bombing us? If not, I don't want to hear it."

"Yeah, you do. They're saying Senator Webster had some extra-marital affairs and the women are going to come forward to confirm it. I heard it on the FOX network this afternoon. How's that going to play out tomorrow night?"

"Jesus! Are you sure it's Senator Webster?"

"Yes, I'm sure. The senator wasn't available for comment. You have to wonder if Dr. Webster knows. Maybe she knows all about it and that's why she's spending so much time at Pinewood. Women consoling women. That kind of thing. Maybe that's why she wasn't anxious to go in the house. I bet she knows."

"We'll talk in the morning. I need to think about what you just told me. By the way, what did you find on Charles Martin?"

"Give me a break, Jack. I was going to work on that when I got home. My home computer is tied into the one at the office. You have me going in six different directions. I can tell you this, the guy didn't exist prior to his employment at the Rutledge candy company. I did get that far."

"What the hell does that mean, Mark?"

"It means your guy doesn't have a background. No trace of him up to the day he started to work as head of security at the Rutledge business. I'll check Interpol. I have a few contacts abroad. Listen, I'm home. We can talk in the morning."

"Wait a minute, Mark. Run a check on Myra, too, way back to when she was born, OK?"

"Sure, why was I stupid enough to think I need sleep."

Ten minutes later, Jack parked his car in the first parking space he could find. He needed to think about what Mark had just said. He racked his brain as he made his way to his apartment in the pouring rain to remember everything Nikki had ever said about Myra's live-in companion. The only thing he could come up with was Charles should be anointed for sainthood. He was a gourmet cook, he loved Myra and Nikki and he had loved Barbara, too. He ran security at the candy plant. He had all kinds of talents. He knew Myra when they were young. Myra had gone to England with her father, and they met and fell in love, and then something went awry. What went awry? Did Nik ever tell him? If she did, he couldn't remember.

Was Charles British? For some reason, he thought so. He'd been in his company twice to his knowledge. Did the man speak? Shit, he couldn't remember. He should know that. Yeah, yeah, he was British. Nik said he made Beef Wellington all the time but no one liked it but

Charles. He liked to drink PIM's too, a British drink.

Screw it all, he was going to bed. Tomorrow was another day.

Eight

Out of sorts, unsure what was bothering him, Mark Lane changed into dry clothes and took his place at the computer. He polished his glasses, cracked his knuckles and stared at the blank screen in front of him. All he could see was the fear on Dr. Julia Webster's face as she prepared to enter her house where Senator Webster awaited her.

Dr. Julia Webster wasn't his business or FBI business. All he'd done was help out an old college buddy who had a few screws loose.

Mark cracked his knuckles again. He was no longer a field agent due to a heart attack at the young age of thirty-two. These days he was a desk jockey who ran computer programs for the

Bureau. He missed being in the field which was why he'd agreed to help Jack. What was a little clandestine surveillance? His field instincts were just as good as ever. He hadn't lost those with his surgery. Something was wrong in the Webster household. Maybe Jack wasn't as paranoid as he originally thought.

Mark looked at the time on the bottom window of his computer. Eleven o'clock.

At this hour of the night he could make it to Georgetown in ten minutes. To do what? Stand in the rain and play Peeping Tom?

"I'm going! No, I'm not going out in this rain! Hell, yes, I'm going."

Five minutes later, dressed in one of his FBI slickers, Mark was in the Pathfinder headed toward Georgetown. What he was going to do when he got there, he had no clue.

Julia tried to be quiet, hoping against hope that Mitch was upstairs in bed. Unlikely, since the house was lit up like a Christmas tree. He was probably glued to the television waiting for the eleven o'clock news. He probably had a good bit of liquor under his belt, too. She hated it when Mitch drank to excess because he was an ugly drunk.

In the kitchen, Julia opened the refrigerator and poured herself a glass of orange juice. She carried her glass over to the sink and stared out at the black, rainy night. All she could really see was the gas lamp with its sickly, yellow light shining downward.

She raised her eyes to see Mitch's reflection. He was standing in the doorway wearing the same suit he'd probably started the day with. His tie was askew, his power suit rumpled. In his hand he held a highball glass. Julia turned around but didn't say anything. She waited, her stomach in knots.

"Where the hell have you been, Julia? I called you a hundred times. We need to get on the same page here. Where were you?"

"What page is that, Mitch? I said I would be here to go to the party. Here I am."

"You couldn't wait, could you? You had to run screaming to those slimy reporters and spew your garbage."

Julia sipped at the orange juice. "I did not run screaming to any reporters nor did I spew any garbage. I would never do that to you. What you and I discussed in this house stays between us. I see no need to air our dirty laundry for the gossip mongers of this town. If you're looking to place blame, look somewhere else."

"And you expect me to believe you?" Mitch ranted.

"Yes, Mitch, I do." Julia sipped at the orange juice again. It tasted bitter.

"Well, I don't. No one else knew. You made me write out that goddamn list. Now I know why you wanted me to do that. You need to call those slimy people and retract what you said. This is going to kill me politically."

Better to die politically than to die physically. "You're delusional. I told you I didn't do it, therefore I cannot call and rescind. Look somewhere else. There are a lot of people who hate you in this town and we both know it."

Julia moved across the kitchen to turn on the small flat screen television on the kitchen counter. "Let's see what they have to say," she said quietly. *His eyes are getting mean. He's working up to something.*

They didn't have long to wait. The second sound bite of the night had to do with Senator Webster's supposed dalliance. Julia watched her husband out of the corner of her eye. She could see that Mitch had set his highball glass on the counter and was smacking his clenched fist into his open palm. The venom he was spewing scared her; then a long-legged model type flashed on the screen. She looked to be in her mid-twenties with a wealth of shimmering blonde hair and breasts that couldn't be real. Julia listened to the lie she was telling. For some reason it sounded more of a lie because of her pronounced southern twang. "I have not had any kind of relationship with that man, Senator Webster." Julia almost laughed aloud. Miss Connie McBride was the third name on Mitch's list of paramours. "I'm very flattered but unfortunately, it's just all a vicious lie. The right wing. Y'all know how that works in this town. Now, y'all aren't going to start following me around and hounding me, are you? Now, don't be calling me at all hours of the day and night, ya hear?" She winked seductively at the reporter interviewing her.

Julia's heartbeat quickened. If Connie McBride was third on Mitch's slut list, there was a good chance she was a recent affair, which could well mean she was infected with HIV. Her gaze returned to the television screen where the buxom, long-legged blonde was still pretending to be outraged at having her character besmirched even though she was flattered.

Senator Webster looked absolutely livid as he downed the last of the scotch in his glass in one mighty gulp.

Outside, the rain slashed against the kitchen window as a lightning bolt shot across the sky. An early spring storm, just like the storm going on in this kitchen, Julia thought crazily. Her voice was calm, and it surprised her, when she said, "Now, Mitch, if you can lie as good as that slut you have nothing to worry about. Just for the record, she didn't convince me and she looked guilty as hell. Let's not forget how flattered she is to be coupled with the distinguished senator from Pennsylvania. Those boobs aren't real either."

"Will you shut up. Why would she lie?"

"I can't believe you just said that. You wrote

her goddamn name on the goddam list. She's lying, just the way you lie. Excuse me, lied. I have the list in my purse. She was number three on that list if you recall. It's going to snowball, Mitch."

"You did it to get even with me. I know you did and you stand there looking like some sick saint. What the hell's wrong with you anyway? You look like shit. You have bags and dark circles under your eyes and your hair is like straw. I hope to hell you have some good makeup and a decent dress that won't make you look like a scarecrow for tomorrow night. The cameras are going to be on you all night long."

Julia bit down on her tongue. *Wait and see how you look when this devil illness hits you, you bastard.* She turned to walk away, her shoulders slumped. Then her feet left the floor and Mitch had her under the armpits holding her in the air. "I want an answer, Julia. Why did you turn on me like this? For Christ's sake, they were just affairs, they didn't mean anything. Just about every man in this fucking town is having an affair and if it isn't with a woman it's with another man."

"Take your hands off me. If you don't, I'll call the police and file a domestic abuse report. You wouldn't want that now, would you? You disgust me. I'm not going to tell you again, put me down," Julia screamed.

"You want down, you bitch! I'll show you *down!*' Mitch released his vise-like grip on her, and Julia fell to the floor with such force she literally saw stars. Too stunned to do anything, she started to cry.

"That's it, cry. Bawl your head off. You ruined me. You damn well ruined me!"

"You ruined yourself, you ass. If you had kept your pants zipped, you wouldn't be in this position and I wouldn't be . . . I wouldn't . . ." Julia bit down on her lip. She'd almost blurted out her medical condition. She inched away when she saw Mitch's foot swing out but she wasn't quick enough. She screamed with pain when Mitch's wing tip got her smack in the rib cage.

Outside in the bushes by the kitchen window, Mark Lane took in the situation. He skirted a forsythia bush in bloom and leaped up onto the small stoop that led to the back door where he started to pound at the door. "FBI," he shouted to be heard over the driving rain.

Mitch whirled around, his eyes wild. "What in the damn hell is the FBI doing here?" Julia didn't answer, she just cowered in fear and pain against the sink. "You called in the fucking FBI?"

"No!" Julia whispered. "No, I didn't."

Outside in the pouring rain, Mark kicked at the door. "Open on the count of three or I'll knock this door down!"

Mitch walked over and opened the door. Agent Lane stepped into the kitchen and went immediately to where Julia was crouched in the corner, her face full of pain.

"Let's see some goddamn ID," Mitch blustered.

Mark dug in his shirt pocket and pulled out his credentials. He flashed them as he leaned over to Julia. He was stunned speechless when she said. "Charles sent you in the nick of time. Thank God. Get me out of here before he kills me. Please, take me back to Myra's. I think he cracked my rib cage. Just get me out of here."

Charles. That had to mean this woman wanted him to take her back to Myra Rutledge's estate. She thought Charles Martin sent him. Shit, now he was into something right up to his neck. She was whispering again. "I didn't tell him. I almost did but I knew Charles would have a fit. Oh, God, Oh, God!"

What the hell? "Can you walk, Dr. Webster?"

"I think so. I'll crawl if I have to. Just get me back to Myra and Charles."

Mitch finally found his voice as Agent Lane half carried his wife toward the kitchen door. "Where the hell do you think you're going? I don't give a good rat's ass if you're FBI or not. What was your name again?"

Mark ignored him as he struggled to open the door. "You're going to get wet, Dr. Webster."

"I don't care." Julia shot a look at her husband. "Just take me to the hospital. I'll say I fell off a ladder."

Outside in the pouring rain, Mark found his voice. "I thought you said you wanted me to take you to Myra and Charles. Do you want to go to the hospital instead?"

"No, I just said that so he wouldn't call the FBI. I know you're not a real agent, you're one of Charles's operatives. I don't know how he does it. You arrived at just the right moment. If you told me your name, I can't remember it. I'm sorry. Can you get my medical bag out of the car and the satchel next to it? I need to take some Advil. I should have killed him but he took me by surprise."

Shit! Shit! Shit! She wanted his name. Oh, Emery, I am going to fucking kill you when I get my hands on you. "Tom. Tom Warwick," Mark said as he helped Julia into the Pathfinder. He set the medical bag on her lap and her other bag on the floor.

"I didn't want him to call the FBI because I know . . . Oh, God, I almost blew it and told him I was HIV and he was the one who gave it to me. But then you know all that already. I didn't tell, though, even when he kicked me. He still thinks he can save his career. Listen, I'm sorry you had to witness that scene back in my kitchen. Mitch was so angry, I thought he was going to kill me. Thank God for Charles and his . . . for you and for everyone helping me with this mission," Julia gasped.

Mission? Oh, shit, oh, shit! What the hell is she talking about? First I'm going to torture you, then I'm going to kill you, Emery. Mark made a noise in his throat that he hoped sounded sympathetic as his mind raced. On the other hand, Jack might kill him if he *didn't* ask questions. What the hell should he ask? He grappled with something to say. He finally came up with something brilliant. "So, how is all of the rest of it going?"

"We're on target. You know Charles. He is so brilliant he boggles my mind. Did you work with him when he was MI6? No one ever told us his real name. It probably has something to do with his work as a spy. I guess you know all that, too. I'm just talking to hear myself so I won't think about the pain I'm in."

We're on target. Well, hot damn? He wondered how he could find out what *the target* was. Maybe Jack would know. "No, sorry, he was before my time. But the man is a legend in his own time." Well, that was brilliant. There was so much saliva in his mouth, Mark thought he was going to drown in his own drool.

"You can say that again. God, this hurts. I should have taken some painkillers. It's OK, I have to be careful what kind of meds I take these days. We'd all be dead in the water without Charles. He pulls it all together."

"Yeah, yeah, he's that kind of guy. He knows how to . . . to . . . pull things together. A master." Another brilliant statement but the doctor was buying it.

Mark drove in silence as he racked his brain. How much to say? How much not to say? He wished he could call Jack for instructions.

"Dr. Webster, how long has your husband been . . . abusing you?"

"He's never abused me. Tonight was . . . was the first time. He blames me for leaking his affair with that young woman. His career is ruined. I don't know why he's going to go through with the announcement tomorrow night. We really didn't talk much before you arrived."

"Uh-huh," was all Mark could think of to say. He cautioned himself to say as little as possible so as not to arouse her suspicions. Damn, he could hardly wait to tell all this to Jack. "Are you still planning on going to the armory tomorrow evening? Will you be up to it?"

Julia shifted in her seat. She undid her seat belt and then re-buckled it. "I have to attend. I can't let the others down. We work as a team and they depend on me. Once my ribs are taped up, I'll be OK. No one will think twice about me going by myself. I'm a doctor. Doctors are always late. I always show up at these functions, not necessarily on my husband's arm. Most times I show up when the affair is almost over. That's because I hate all that political nonsense. Tomorrow night, though, the press will read whatever they want to read into my arrival. Charles will have it under control. Besides, Mitch is just part of the mission."

Mark's mouth filled with saliva again. *Holy shit! Part of the mission.* This time he didn't trust himself to even grunt. Finally, he managed to say, "We're almost there, Dr. Webster." This is where I get my ass handed to me on a platter. As soon as miracle worker Charles Martin got him in his crosshairs, he was dead in the water. He'd probably call the local authorities and charge him with impersonating an FBI agent. Hell, he was an FBI agent. If he wasn't so nervous, he would have laughed.

"Thank you, God," Julia said quietly. "Listen, Tom, you'll have to drop me at the gate. I'll walk through. If the dogs don't know you, they'll rip you to pieces. We have a twelve foot high fence to . . . to keep people out. The dogs patrol the fence. We . . . we had an intruder the other night but he was outside the fence. I'll be fine once I get inside. I don't know how to thank you. You saved my life tonight. I never thought . . . I didn't expect . . ."

Saved. He was saved. They weren't going to string him up by his thumbs. *I'm still going to kill you, Jack.* He hoped the exquisite relief he felt didn't show in his voice when he said, "Well, I certainly don't want to . . . you know, screw things up. If you're sure you'll be OK, I'll simply turn around and head for home."

"I'm sure. Thank you again, Tom."

Mark hopped out of the car and ran around to the side and opened the car door for Julia to climb out. When she couldn't do it, he reached in and lifted her out and set her on the ground.

She felt so thin, so fragile. "Look, I can't leave you here like this. What about your bags?"

"Take a look at those dogs by the fence and say that again. Just toss the bags inside when I open the gate. Someone will come out and get them. I'm fine. I hope I can do something for you some day."

Mark watched as Julia keyed in a code and then walked through the gates when they opened. The Dobermans didn't bark but they didn't move either as Julia moved among them. The instant the gates closed, Mark was back in the Pathfinder. He backed up and then spun around and headed away from Pinewood, rain cascading all around him.

Ten miles down the road, Mark was finally able to take a deep breath. What in the hell had he just stepped into? It was a myth that FBI agents had nerves of steel. He was twanging from head to toe. He wanted to call Jack so badly he could taste the feeling but he'd left his cell phone back in his apartment which meant he had to drive to Jack's apartment and wake him up. An evil grin stretched across his face at the pleasure that was going to give him. "Mix me up in your shit and you deserve whatever you get, old buddy," he mumbled.

Twenty minutes later Mark was banging on Jack's door. He kicked at it a few times in between knocks. When the door finally opened he looked at his friend who was dressed in white boxers sprinkled with red hearts. "Wow! Do you always look like this when you wake up?" Mark asked, referring to Jack's overlong hair that was standing on end, his unshaven face, hairy chest and skinny legs. "No wonder Nikki dumped you. You'd scare the devil in the morning."

"I should kill you right now but I don't know where my gun is. Do you know what time it is? Did the J Edgar Hoover building blow up or something? What? Speak." Jack growled menacingly as he eyeballed his friend.

Mark shoved Jack backward and headed for the kitchen where he opened the refrigerator and uncapped a Michelob. He took a long swig before he spoke. "The building is still standing, thank you very much. This is better. Sit down, Jack, because if you don't, I'm going to deck you. What the hell is this shit you got me mixed up in? I don't think you covered the half of it."

"I told you all I know and everything I suspect. What happened? Don't make me beat it out of you, Mark."

Mark repeated the night's events right up to the point where his tires spun on the gravel outside the gates of Pinewood. "I just left her there. I felt like shit doing that but I wasn't about to take on a pack of Dobermans and besides, she insisted."

"No one dies of broken ribs. I never liked Senator Webster. All he does is talk so he can show off his pricey porcelain. Never would have figured him for a wife beater. Are you sure Dr. Webster . . ."

"Jack, I'm sure. She thought Charles Martin sent me. Hey, I announced myself when I banged on their back door. The senator wanted to see ID and I flashed it. In case you haven't noticed, I am wearing my FBI windbreaker. You'd have to be blind to miss those big yellow letters but I was smart enough to give a phony name. Just call me Tom Warwick."

Jack hitched up his boxers and then scratched the stubble on his chin. "She actually used the word mission?"

"Several times as a matter of fact. She assumed I knew what was going on. I did my best to act like I knew. I never felt so clueless in my life. The woman is sick, Jack. I picked her up and she weighs nothing. I wanted to do something, say something, but I didn't know what to do. I thought about going back there before I came here to deck that bastard but common sense brought me here instead. She got infected from her husband who she has kept in the dark for some reason. From what she said and didn't say, the senator doesn't know he's HIV. Tell me this isn't some heavy duty stuff. How does all this fit together with what you've been saying and thinking, Jack?"

"It's the word, mission, that's boggling my

mind. Maybe they're setting the senator up for something. They leak his infidelities to the press and boom, his nomination goes down the tubes. He's ruined. Then there's good old Charles. MI6, huh? See, now, that puts a whole other spin on things.

"Mission. MI6. Myra Rutledge's wealth. Seven women. All strangers to one another until they hired Nikki. Nikki is the catalyst. I guess you didn't hear from your friend at Interpol, huh?"

"I was kind of busy, Jack. I was going to work the computer but I couldn't get the doctor's face out of my mind, so I went back there. I'm going home now and going to bed. All right, all right, I'll send off an E-mail before I sack out. I can't go on adrenaline like you do. Thanks for the beer," Mark said, tossing the empty bottle to his friend who caught it by the long neck.

"Thanks, Mark. I'll see you at three-thirty. You did real good tonight. I owe you for this."

"Don't think I'm going to forget it either," Mark snapped as he let himself out of the apartment.

All the way back to his apartment he could only think about Dr. Julia Webster. He hoped she would be all right. Then he started to worry. Did the security monitors pick up his license plate when he was turning the car around? He wasn't sure but he thought he backed up far enough so that he was outside the ray of light over the keypad before he swung the Pathfinder down the drive and then out to the highway.

Maybe he wasn't going to sleep after all. Maybe he needed to call Ambrose Coxney instead of E-mailing him. No point in leaving a paper trail. He could always take a nap later on.

Mark let himself into his apartment. From long years of training, he stood in the open doorway and looked around trying to see if anyone had entered his apartment while he was gone. The peanut shell was still where he'd left it by the front door. The pencil was still lying across his keyboard, the eraser pointed toward the Backspace key. He nodded in satisfaction as he headed for his bedroom and his shower. When he returned to his spare bedroom turned office, he was wearing pajamas and slippers. His receding hair was slicked back and his wire rimmed glasses were polished. He reached for an apple and a box of crackers to fortify himself as he logged on to his computer. He needed a picture of Charles Martin to forward to Ambrose. He remembered seeing one on the Rutledge Candy Company Web site. It was taken when Charles Martin signed on as new chief of security at the factory years and years ago. With luck, Ambrose could match it up from his side of the pond to Martin's dossier when he was with MI6.

As his mouse clicked and clicked, Mark realized Jack was on to something serious.

Myra was about to turn off the kitchen light and follow Charles upstairs. The others had retired earlier, leaving them alone to share a late night cup of tea. Out of the corner of her eye, she could see movement on the monitor by the security gates. "Charles, someone is coming *through* the gate. Who is it, dear?" She ran to the door to peer out in the rain. "It's Julia! Quickly, Charles, something's wrong." Before Charles could get up from the table, Myra was running outside and across the lawn to where Julia was staggering toward her. Myra caught her in her arms just as Charles arrived.

Charles reached out and scooped Julia up in his arms. She moaned in pain. Like Mark Lane, he was stunned at how little she weighed.

Inside, Myra ran to the laundry room for towels and blankets. She returned in time to hear Julia say, "He was so livid, he lifted me off the ground and started punching me. Then he put me down and kicked me in the ribs. Your operative arrived just in time and got me out of there. He wanted to take me to the hospital, but I told him to bring me here. Just tape me up, Charles. I took some Advil but I need some more. I don't want to mix my meds with painkillers. Even if I went to the hospital, all they would do is take an x-ray and I'd have to lie through my teeth. Mitch thinks I went to the hospital. I told him I would say I fell. At that point I would have said or done anything to get out of there. I think I'd like some brandy, Charles."

Myra moved out of Julia's eye range, her hand fluttering, panic written all over her face. She needed both hands to grasp the brandy bottle. In the end, she got more of the plum brandy on the counter than she did in the glass.

Charles worked quickly, taping her ribs, then sliding a soft T-shirt over her head. He held Julia in his arms as she sipped at the fiery liquid. Her eyes watered at the onslaught on her throat. Exhausted, she leaned back. "It feels so much better with the tape. It doesn't hurt to breathe. Stop worrying, Charles, I'm a doctor. I'll be fine. I wouldn't be so fine if your man hadn't showed up when he did. Mitch was . . . he was so . . . so violent. He saw the eleven o'clock news and that's when he turned on me."

Charles released his hold on Julia and walked deeper into the kitchen so Myra could dress Julia in warm clothing. He was as close to panic as he'd ever been in his life. What in the name of God was Julia talking about? What operative of his had intervened?

He galloped up the back stairway and ran down the hall to Nikki's room. He knocked and then entered. She was sound asleep. He shook her gently. "Shhh, it's me, Charles. I need to talk with you."

Nikki reared back and sat up, her eyes frightened. "What's wrong? Don't tell me something happened to Myra. Please, Charles, don't tell me that."

"No, no, it's not Myra. It's Julia." He quickly recounted what had just happened. "I don't know, Nikki. Maybe it was Jack. I don't think she's ever met him so how could she know? She's so fragile and she's in a lot of pain. I don't want to frighten her so I thought you and Myra could sit with her and get the whole story out of her. She's going to be devastated when she realizes the man who saved her isn't one of our people. The best we can hope for right now is she didn't give up anything. Hurry, Nikki, before she drops off to sleep. I need to know what we're up against."

Nikki bolted from the bed and raced downstairs, her heart pumping in fear.

"Julia, Julia, I am so sorry. Is there anything I can do?" Nikki asked, dropping to her knees beside the sofa where Julia was lying. Myra sat cross-legged on the floor, holding Julia's hand.

"I'm OK, Nikki. I'm going to be stiff and sore for a few days but I will make it tomorrow night. I just won't be going with Mitch." Her eyes drooped and then closed.

Nikki watched as Myra threw a light blanket over Julia. "What did she say?" Nikki whispered.

Myra motioned Nikki to follow her out to the kitchen where Charles was waiting for them. His eyes were full of questions. Both women shrugged. "She's sleeping, Charles. I didn't have the heart to question her. Morning will be soon enough."

"No, Myra, morning won't be soon enough. We have to get on top of this right now. Otherwise, we have to postpone tomorrow night's activities."

"It's the middle of the night, dear. What can we possibly do other than wake up Julia?"

"Julia is bound to stir eventually. I want you both to sit with her. The moment she opens her eyes, question her. I'll be in the command center. What bothers me is that she never met Jack Emery. It could have been Jack who rescued her. Julia did say the man said he was from the FBI and very nice. She said the letters, FBI were on the back of his windbreaker."

Nikki turned off the stove and filled three cups with water and tea bags. Something tugged at her, something she should be remembering. She twirled the tea bag in her cup, frowning. FBI. Who did she know in the FBI. No one. Who did Jack know in the FBI? "Oh, my God! Mark Lane!" The agent had stopped by their table once when she and Jack were at McGuire's.

At Charles and Myra's startled looks, she explained. "Jack has a friend who's an agent at the FBI. I met him once. Nice guy. Kind of sad, though. He had a heart attack shortly after he joined the FBI. He was a field agent, a good one, too, according to Jack. After his recovery he became a computer programmer. Maybe Jack . . . I'm reaching here, Charles, but maybe Jack enlisted his help. I can tell Julia what he looks like. If it was Mark, we're in trouble."

"I'll see what I can come up with on Agent Lane. I might be able to get a picture. Do you know where he went to college or where his hometown is?" Charles asked.

"I don't know where he's from but he went to Duke University with Jack. It was a long time ago, Charles. I just have a foggy memory of it. I more or less homed in on the fact that a young guy like him had a heart attack. I'm sorry, Charles."

"No, no, that's perfectly understandable. The fact that you remembered at all is a tremendous help. Come to the command center if Julia wakes and tell me what she says."

Myra sipped at the herbal tea and eyed Nikki over the rim of her cup. "How . . . how serious is all this, Nikki?"

Nikki wished there was something she could say to drive the worry from Myra's eyes but there wasn't. "About as serious as it gets. I guess it's time to do something about Jack before he involves someone else. I don't know if we have any other choice, Myra."

"I am so sorry, dear. I wish . . . oh, Lord, I wish so many things. If you want to . . ."

"Stop right there, Myra. I'm not going to back out of the Sisterhood because of Jack Emery. We just have to find a way to deal with him that will work to our advantage."

"Can he be bought? A bribe?"

"Don't even go there, Myra. The short answer is, no. Jack has an ego and that ego has been bruised by a bunch of women. It's not that he's against women or anything like that, but he goes by the book, it's black or white. There are no gray areas where Jack is concerned. He lives for the law. At least he did. In a million years he would never be able to deal with what we're doing. He wants us locked up and the key thrown away. And, don't forget, he's been called on the carpet, courtesy of the governor's call to the police commissioner on your behalf. Last but not least, he's bent out of shape because he thinks I chose you over him." Nikki threw her hands in the air to show what she thought of that particular statement.

Nikki eyed her adopted mother who looked exhausted. "Myra, go to bed. You haven't had any sleep yet. It's going to be a busy day and night. You need some rest. I've had a few hours sleep so I'll sit with Julia. I need to do some deep thinking. It's all doable, Myra, so don't be worried. If I need you, I'll call you."

"All right, dear. You're right about me needing some sleep. I'm sorry but I do worry. I feel so terrible about you and Jack. I wish . . . never mind, good night, dear. Be sure to call me if you need me."

"I promise. I'll check in on Charles in a bit." Nikki allowed herself to be hugged before she waved good night.

Nikki made fresh tea and carried it into the den where Julia was still sleeping on the sofa. She stared down at her friend and wondered how she herself would handle what Julia was going through if the situation was reversed. I'd probably be a raving lunatic, she thought. She sat down, mumbling a prayer for Julia that somehow, some way, a miracle would happen for her.

Nikki's mind raced as she sipped at her tea and struggled to come up with a solution to what was going on in her life. Eventually, because she was tired, she dozed off to be awakened hours later when she heard Julia whisper her name. "I need to use the bathroom, Nikki. Can you help me get up?"

Both women were back on the sofa minutes later. The clock on the mantel said it was four o'clock in the morning. "I'm all right, Nikki. I'm sore but that's to be expected. Can you get my cell phone out of my bag? I want to see if Mitch called."

Nikki rummaged in Julia's bag until she found the phone. She watched as Julia pressed a series of numbers to pick up her messages. A look of pure fury replaced the pain in her face as she suddenly threw the small phone across the room. "Typical, Mitch, threaten and intimidate when he doesn't get his way. He *demands* that I come home. Like that's really going to happen."

"Tell me what happened, Julia. Don't leave anything out. We need to get a handle on all of this before tonight." Nikki leaned back in her chair, her legs tucked beneath her. The scene could have passed for a girls' sleepover where telling secrets was the order of the day.

"The eleven o'clock news came on and this woman, Connie McBride, who was number three on Mitch's slut list, appeared. She denied having an affair with the distinguished senator from Pennsylvania but she was flattered nonetheless. Do you believe that? Maybe late twenties, married to a first term congressman. Long legs, artificial boobs, blonde. Beautiful. Any man would be attracted to her. Compared to her, I look like a down and out bag lady without even a cardboard box to sleep in.

"Mitch and I had words. Before I knew it, he grabbed me under the arms and lifted me off

171

the floor. He's really strong. We were screaming at one another. I told him to put me down, and he just . . . he just dropped me. I literally saw stars. Then he kicked me. It would have been worse but I moved when I realized his intent. The pain really rocked me.

"I couldn't believe it when there was a knock on the kitchen door and the man said, open up, FBI, or something like that. I knew instantly that it wasn't the FBI but one of Charles's people. Mitch didn't know that, though. He asked for ID, and this guy Tom showed him his badge or whatever agents carry around. I was in so much pain I wasn't paying too much attention.

"Agent Warwick picked me up and I told him to take me to the hospital—that was just for Mitch's benefit. Just seconds before I whispered for him to bring me here and he said OK. He was so nice, Nikki. So concerned. I had the feeling it was all he could do not to punch Mitch out. He really did want to take me to the hospital."

Nikki's heart fluttered in her chest. "I want you to think very carefully, Julia. What exactly did the agent say and what did you say to him? Exactly, Julia."

A flicker of fear showed in Julia's eyes. She clutched the light blanket with both hands. "I did most of the talking. Agent Warwick . . . that's what he said his name was, was concentrating on his driving. The weather was terrible. I was babbling. I was so upset, Nikki. We talked about Charles. I kept saying I was so grateful Charles had sent him and he arrived at just the right moment. We talked about Charles being in Her Majesty's service. I said I didn't even know what his British name was. He said Charles was a legend in his own time but it was before his time. That kind of thing."

"Did you mention tonight's activities?" Nikki asked carefully.

"Yes. I talked about the mission, he seemed to understand and didn't ask any questions. Why, Nikki? You're starting to scare me."

"Tell me what he looked like. Did you have to give him directions out here?"

"No, he knew the way. He was plain-looking, sandy hair, receding a little. Young—and by young I mean maybe mid thirties. He was wearing an FBI windbreaker. The letters were big and yellow on the back. He wasn't fat but he was a little overweight for his height, which was about five-eleven or so. He was extremely competent and I felt safe with him. He seemed more concerned with my well-being than anything I said. I don't know, Nikki, I was in a lot of pain and gulping Advil. Say it, say I screwed up."

"You screwed up, Julia, but I probably would have done the same thing. The person you described is not anyone any of us knows. Charles did not send him. At first we thought it was Jack but Jack is tall and movie star handsome. I think the person who saved you is a friend of Jack's and his name is Mark Lane. I met him once when I was with Jack. You're right, he's a nice guy. The description you just gave me fits Mark. What happened when you got to the gates?"

Julia groaned, her head dropping to her hands. "I told him to let me out because of the dogs. He seemed . . . relieved. I don't know if this means anything but instead of turning around, he backed way down the road before he turned around. I thought that was strange but now when I think about it, I guess he didn't want the camera to pick up his license plate on the back. It was a Pathfinder. Nikki, I am so sorry. It was the jacket, the nick of time save. I have to tell Charles."

"You stay right there and rest and don't beat yourself up over this. Being forewarned will keep us from walking into an ambush. Charles is in the command center. He'll know what to do. The others are sleeping. I'll make us all some coffee."

Julia beat at the pillow with her clenched fists as tears rolled down her cheeks.

In the kitchen, Nikki zipped around running water, filling the pot, pouring in coffee grounds and getting out cream and sugar before she raced through the house to the secret war room.

"We're in the brown stuff, Charles. Julia didn't quite give it up but she said enough so that when Mark Lane goes back to Jack, he's going to know. She told him about you and Her Majesty and Lane said you were a legend in your own time even though you were before his time. Seems he knows about you or else he pretended. She pretty much hinted at the mission and used that exact word. She's devastated, Charles. What should we do? What *can* we do? I'm making coffee."

Nikki had never seen Charles ruffled but he was ruffled now. It frightened her.

"Coffee sounds good, Nikki. I'd like it black with a shot of brandy in it. Is Julia all right and is Myra sleeping?'

Nikki felt even more frightened with Charles's order for coffee. He always took heavy cream and four sugars. "OK on the coffee. Yes, Myra is sleeping and no, Julia is not all right. Considering the situation, I tend to think I might have reacted the same way she did."

"Yes, yes. I understand. I'm not blaming her. We just have to fall back and regroup. I need to . . . hurry with the coffee, Nikki."

Nikki trotted off. "I should kill you, Jack. At the very least, incapacitate you for a good long while," she muttered to herself as she prepared Charles's coffee. Her shoulders slumped when she returned yet again to the kitchen to prepare coffee for Julia and herself. Jack was an officer of the court, doing what he was supposed to do. She and the others were breaking the law. No matter how she sliced and diced it, the Sisterhood was in the wrong. Jack was in the right. In her heart of hearts, she couldn't blame him for listening to his instincts and acting on those instincts. The big question was, if things got down and dirty, would she be able to go along with her sisters to do something drastic to the man she loved. Or would she break all the rules and warn Jack. It was going to come to that; she could feel it in her bones. Which way would she turn? Right now, right this very moment, she didn't have an answer.

"Want some more Advil, Julia?" Nikki asked, setting the coffee cup down on the cocktail table. "Would you rather be alone or do you want to talk?" she asked gently.

Julia grimaced. "I think I already talked too much, Nikki. What did Charles say? How upset is he with me?"

"Julia, Charles understands. We all understand. He's working on it. Knowing Charles as well as I do, I think we're still on for this evening. There will be some changes but we're going to pull it off. Hey, we're women! We can do anything if we put our minds to it. Remember, there were some glitches during Kathryn's mission. We pulled it off and no one was the wiser."

Julia struggled to find a more comfortable sitting position. "Jack and his new partner know too much, Nikki."

"Yes, I know. They could do real damage to Charles and his new identity here in this country. If you want to know what my secret fear is, it's that Charles will tell his people on the other side of the pond and they will take care of Jack and Mark."

Julia clutched one of Myra's needlepoint pillows to her chest. Tears trickled down her drawn cheeks. "Oh, God, I didn't think of that, Nikki. Will they . . . will they . . ." Julia couldn't bring herself to finish what Nikki was thinking.

"I don't know. I think so. That covert spy stuff by both governments is serious stuff. We're babes in the woods compared to what those guys do. I suppose it's possible they could arrange *to talk* to Mark and Jack." Nikki shivered as she crossed her arms over her chest.

"The FBI and the Secret Service will be at the armory this evening. I'm surprised Mitch doesn't have an all points out on me. If he doesn't withdraw or tell the governor he doesn't want to be his running mate, I'm fair game from here on in. I'll be under a microscope."

"Charles is working on it, Julia. Right now, I'm concerned about you. Can you take a shower? I'll help you."

"It doesn't matter if I should or shouldn't. I'm going to do it. I got caught in the rain twice yesterday. You can help me wash my hair if you don't mind. Then you'll have to re-tape my ribs. I . . . I want to look as nice as I can this evening. Mitch said some ugly things to me that I will never forget. I guess he hasn't taken a good look at me lately. He was very cruel. I can't forgive him for that. You know, Nikki, I almost blurted it all out but I bit my tongue so hard I drew blood. I was married to that man for God's sake. Why didn't I ever do something? Why did I stay? What's wrong with me?"

Nikki held out her hands, dug her heels into the carpeting and pulled Julia to her feet. Together they made their way to the downstairs bathroom where Nikki got out towels, soap, and shampoo. "Hot, warm or cool?"

"Hot. I can adjust it after I stand under the steam." Julia stood still as Nikki helped her undress.

Nikki held her tears until Julia stepped into the shower. She wiped at her eyes on the sleeve of her pajamas. When it was time for her to make a decision where Jack and Mark were concerned, all she would have to do was remember this moment. Julia deserved her revenge.

Charles paced his domain as he waited for his secure cell phone to ring. After all these years he was in danger again. Like the CIA in Langley, MI6 never slept. What was taking so long? Why weren't they calling him back? He looked into his coffee cup and was surprised to see it empty. He had no clear recollection of finishing it. He started to pace again, the empty cup in his hands.

Dear God, what if MI6 insisted on moving him. Well, that simply wasn't an option. If that was their decision he might have to go over their head to Lizzie. The mere thought of having to do that gave him indigestion. He couldn't leave Myra and the girls. They needed him, depended on him. He could make *Lizzie* understand that. No, leaving his little family was not an option.

The phone rang. Charles clicked on the button knowing his conversation could not be heard by anyone in the world except the person he was talking to.

The voice on the other end of the line apologized for the short delay in not getting back to him sooner. "I'm sorry, Sir Malcolm, but I had to boot this up about nine levels to get you the person you need to speak with. Hold while I transfer this call."

Charles drummed his fingers on the desk in front of him. "Sir Malcolm, Rodney Abernathy here. I caught your call. I don't see a problem. We'll take care of it. Would you like to move on to a warmer climate?"

Charles felt light-headed with relief. He wouldn't have to go to Lizzie after all. "Not at all, Rodney. I just want to be reassured."

"Rest easy, Sir Malcolm. We fielded a call a

short while ago from Interpol. One of your FBI agents imposed on a friendship to make inquiries. There are so many red flags on your file, the man went to his superior. Everything has been taken care of. Is there anything else I can help you with today, Sir Malcolm?"

"No. Thank you. I'll stay in touch should things change." Charles clicked off the phone. How strange to hear himself called Sir Malcolm. His birth name was Malcolm Sutcliff. Lizzie herself had given him his new name when he was sent to America and he'd grown over the years to believe he really was Charles Martin.

Charles felt his shoulders straighten. He had work to do. Lots of work. But first he needed a gallon of coffee to jump-start his adrenaline again. Good Lord, he must have become Americanized along the way. A relieved smile on his face, Charles decided it wasn't a bad thing.

Shortly before the noon hour, the foursome were ready to tee off when the director of the CIA felt his secure mobile phone vibrate inside his shirt pocket. His golfing buddies, the senior senator from Illinois, the Speaker of the House and the FBI's second in command groaned as one. The director clicked on his phone and walked away so his conversation couldn't be overheard. He listened, the expression on his face going from furious to livid to murderous. "Yes, I do recall a similar situation where you did what we requested with no repercussions. I'll see to it. You can assure Her Majesty your man is safe and there will be no need to move him to another location. Of course, I'll get back to you. I'll take care of it as soon as I hang up." The director waved off his friends and headed back to the clubhouse.

Inside his car, his chauffeur standing outside, the director made his first call. It wasn't *that* unusual for the director of the CIA to call the director of the FBI but it wasn't quite normal either. The two men exchanged guarded pleasantries before the CIA got down to business. "Now means now, Adam. They tell me on the other side of the pond that this is crucial. Can you hog-tie your man and his friend? I just want to be sure, Adam. The *lady* across the pond is in a pissy mood from what I gather. No sense in riling her up any further. The fact that the PM isn't involved shows how serious this is. I'll return the favor, Adam, should the occasion arise. Call me when you have something to report. I'm ten minutes late teeing off. Oh, you're on the ninth. I heard about that hole in one you got a few weeks back." The connection ended and the cell phone went back into the director's pocket. Ten minutes later, he said, "OK, boys, what are we betting today?"

* * *

A light misty rain was falling outside as Mark Lane tugged at his tie. He straightened the Windsor knot, looked at himself again to make sure he looked professional, checked his watch to make sure he had plenty of time to pick up Jack Emery. More than enough time. They'd be outside in the rain, and he'd probably catch a cold. One of those spring-summer colds that lingered for weeks. Just the thought depressed him.

Time to warm up the coffee in his cup. Maybe he should eat something. He knew he'd never get a chance to get even close to the buffet table with the delectable tidbits the governor would be serving at this particular bash. Been there, done that.

As Mark waited for the countdown on the microwave he realized he was not looking forward to the evening even though it meant he was "out in the field" so to speak.

A sharp knock startled him just as the microwave beeped signaling his coffee was ready. It must be Jack, so anxious he drove over here to cut down on driving time. Coffee cup in hand, he marched to the door and didn't bother to check the peephole to see who it was. He was about to offer up some kind of blistering comment until he saw the two men standing facing him. His mother hadn't raised any fools. He knew trouble when he saw it. The coffee cup in his hand started to shake.

"Agent Lane?" one of the men said.

Mark blinked as his right eye started to twitch. "Yes. What can I do for you?"

"For starters, you can invite us in unless you want your neighbors knowing your business," the second man said as he flashed his credentials.

Mark stepped aside to allow the two men to enter his apartment. Coffee sloshed out of his cup onto the floor. He ignored it and he used both hands to steady the cup.

"Going somewhere, Agent Lane?"

"The fact that you're standing here tells me probably not. I was going to the armory. I signed on for the extra detail. You can check with my boss."

"We already did, Agent Lane. You're right, you are not going to the armory. Where's your buddy, Jack Emery?"

"Probably home. I was supposed to pick him up."

"That's not going to happen either, Agent Lane. Call him and tell him something came up and he has to drive over here. In the spirit of co-operation. That's all you say, Agent Lane. You say another word and I'll shoot you on the spot."

Mark looked down at his shoes that he'd polished earlier to a high sheen. He could feel his back start to stiffen. "I think I want to know what this is all about. I don't work for you. What does Jack Emery have to do with anything?" *Stupid ass question.*

Mark's thoughts were faster than speeding bullets. He liked his job. No, he loved his job. He had good health benefits which he needed. He didn't need any black marks on his sheet. Still, how could he in good conscience turn Jack over to these guys, and that's exactly what he would be doing if he called him? Plus, Jack was on a thirty day leave without pay. Technically, that made him a civilian. *I knew I should have killed you, Jack.*

"We don't have to tell you squat, Agent Lane," the first man said quietly. Mark heard the menace in his voice. "Make the call."

Mark walked through the living room and down a short hall to his second bedroom that was a home office. He sloshed coffee all the way. He sat down on his swivel chair because he was scared out of his wits. He dialed Jack's number from memory. The second man reached over and pressed the speaker phone button. Jack's voice came across loud and exceptionally clear.

"If this is you, Agent Lane, telling me you changed your mind, I'll come over there and personally kick your ass all the way to New York. What?" he barked.

"Something came up, Jack. Drive over here. I'll be ready to . . . to leave when you get here."

"All right, all right. You fibbies are the pits, you know that. You're so disorganized I have to wonder how you get anything done. Plus today is Saturday, your day off."

"I didn't say it was work related, Jack. All I said was something came up."

The first man pressed a button and the call ended. Mark replaced the phone. He brought the cup to his lips, stunned to see he'd lost the contents. Shit, now he was going to get ants. He tried to take a deep breath and made a horrible sound in his throat. Neither man looked concerned.

"How long will it take Mr. Emery to get here?"

"Depending on traffic, maybe fifteen minutes. If he hits the right lights, ten minutes." Mark continued to hack and sputter. Both men walked back to the living room. Mark followed and sat down in his favorite chair. He'd seen pictures of the shields both these men carried but on a wide screen at a briefing. The instructor at the academy had said in any given year, maybe three such shields were issued by the president of the United States. One year, the instructor said, there had been four. One year, none. What that meant to the students was, if you ever come across someone carrying that particular shield you immediately stand down and turn over everything to the person carrying the shield. The instructor had droned on to say that MI6,

Interpol and the Mossad had similar shields. All were compatible which meant the holders of the shields worked in harmony.

Mark thought about the call he'd made to his friend at Interpol. *Bastard. See if I ever do anything for you.*

The minutes ticked by. Mark finally got up and replenished his coffee. He drank it cold. All the while he wondered where his next assignment was going to be if they didn't fire or kill him. He didn't even want to think about what they'd do to Jack. He remembered his old instructor saying the guys with the special shields were meaner than cat shit, and worse than hired assassins. All the students, including himself, had laughed when he said they shoot first and take names later.

The knock on the door sounded impatient. Neither man said a word as Mark trudged forward.

"C'mon, c'mon, open up, Mark. Let's get this show on the road," Jack bellowed from his side of the door.

Mark opened the door and watched in horror as Jack was literally lifted off the floor and thrown across the room with such force he made a thumping sound when he landed on the sofa. He wondered giddily, how they'd managed to gauge the distance so he didn't crash through the glass topped coffee table. Then again, maybe it was just pure dumb luck.

Mark stared at his friend. He'd seen normal fear, abnormal fear and then the kind of fear he was seeing on Jack's face in his earlier years in the line of duty. *Oh, shit. This is where the rubber meets the road. Keep your mouth shut, buddy, and maybe, just maybe, we can get out of this with our skin intact.*

Nine

Alexis hopped on the bed and clapped her hands for silence. "Yo! Listen up everyone and get in line. Who wants to be first?" She jumped off the bed, to land with a thud next to Yoko. She eyed the Asian with a practiced eye.

"Might I say I do admire those new boobs of yours. I think I can say I've never seen a four foot eight, eighty-five pound female with a set of thirty-six-inch knockers."

Yoko preened and then pranced around Alexis's bedroom. "My husband loves them. Thanks to Julia's colleague, I was able to have it done. No charge. How do you say, complimentary?"

"Wow!" Kathryn grinned. "Do they feel the same?"

Yoko giggled. "My husband says they do. He said he likes it that I am an experimental, progressive woman. Free!"

Julia felt the need to explain. "A colleague of mine has an intern who needed the practice. We did it after hours. I was in the clinic when they were done. Good job if I do say so myself."

It was just enough conversation to defuse the tension in the room before Alexis got down to work. Her famous Red Bag was voluminous and no one was permitted to touch the contents but Alexis herself. The others called her a magician because she could transfer any likeness to something totally different from when she started, with the aid of latex, spirit gum, makeup and costume.

"Who am I going to be this evening?" Yoko gurgled as she gave her new boobs an uplift bounce.

Alexis looked down at the chart Charles had given her prior to all of them retiring to her room to *get ready* for the evening's festivities. "It says here I am to make you three inches taller, pile your hair on your head for added height and transform you into a beautiful regal Chinese royal." She looked Yoko up and down. "I don't know if I can do that. Those boobs are going to throw me off. Besides, you're already beautiful."

At Yoko's crestfallen look, she hastened to add, "I'm teasing, dipshit."

Alexis began taking things out of the over-sized Red Bag, grateful for all the backstage training she'd had when she worked in Little Theater.

The gig was on.

As Alexis pinched and prodded, glued and pasted, her brushes and fingers moving like magic, the others chattered nonstop, mostly to Julia as they clustered around her, offering support.

Nikki looked up from her nest of pillows on the bed. "Are we all clear on every single detail?"

"Got it down pat, Nikki. Wait till you guys see the job Yoko and I did at that armory. It looks like a rainbow. One of the governor's people actually came out to thank us. Gave me a fifty buck tip and winked at me. Yoko got a hundred bucks. I haven't been able to figure that out," Kathryn groused.

"There's going to be a thousand people there this evening and that doesn't count the press," Isabelle said. "Charles said the expected donation was a thousand bucks each. He gave me our checks earlier to distribute. No grass is growing under the nominee's feet on this one. Announcement, pony up, and get the hell out of there. Whatever you do, girls, do not, I repeat, do not forget to bring your invitation. Charles did a masterful job of duplicating them."

"Ta-da!" Alexis said dramatically.

"Oh, myyyy, God!" the women squealed.

"You look like . . ." Kathryn struggled for words and was unable to come up with any. Murphy, who was on the bed with Nikki, reared back and howled.

"Let me save you the trouble and let's go with high priced Asian slut with family ties to the Ming family! The Monarch family will be dying to make my acquaintance." Yoko giggled as she strutted around the room in her underwear.

"I can go with that," Kathryn guffawed. "Girl, when you get that dress on you are going to turn every head in the armory."

The surgeon in Julia leaned over to inspect Yoko's face, trying to see what Alexis had accomplished without the aid of a scalpel. Her cheekbones were higher, her chin more defined. Her face was no longer round but elongated. The dark eyes were now a startling blue. Her nose that had been on the small side was now defined, the nostrils flaring dramatically. Her long, black, silky hair was swirled and coiled on top of her head and held in place with two ivory picks. "My dear, you would put Mata Hari to shame."

"Thank you, Julia. I have to practice walking now in these outrageous shoes. I hope I don't kill myself."

The hours ticked by while Alexis worked her magic on the others. "I deserve a medal for this! Now if you don't mind, I need to work on myself. Someone should call Myra and Charles to see if they approve."

"I'll do it," Nikki said as she pulled on a robe and left the room.

When the door closed behind Nikki, the women started chattering again and as usual the talk centered on men.

"That lets me out," Julia said as she relaxed under Alexis's spell. "Make me look like something other than a walking cadaver."

Alexis pretended to swat her the way the others pretended not to hear Julia's comment. "When I'm done with you, you are going to be one ravishing, kick ass broad. Now, pucker up and let me get to work. If you get tired or if you just want to get up and walk around, let me know and we can take a break. It's not going to take me long to work on myself. I'll look like a long-legged Diana Ross in ten minutes." No one doubted her for a minute.

Another hour wore on as Julia dozed off and on in her chair. The others kept looking at her, hoping she'd make it through the night. No one realized how quiet it was until Julia opened one eye and smiled. "Stop worrying about me. I can do this. If I couldn't, I wouldn't be here. I'll hold up my end. I know exactly what my role is and I won't let you down. You're all so kind to be so concerned. It's been years since anyone really cared about what happened to me. You're my family now. I'll do my share this evening. Ohhh, I can't wait to put on that gown. I can't remember the last time I got really dressed to the nines."

The women relaxed but the concern stayed in their eyes. They would all look out for her during the evening. That was a given.

"What's the latest on Jack Emery? Does anyone know?" Yoko asked.

Alexis stopped what she was doing and said, "Charles was like a scalded cat when the stuff hit the fan. Then he turned into a pussy cat so that tells me Myra's call to the governor took care of things."

Yoko moved to the center of the room in her spike heeled, platform shoes and said, "Men like Jack Emery do not give up. He will find a way. What is that saying Americans have? Yes, yes, he marches to his own drummer. He will find a way to intrude into our lives again. That means we must always be vigilant. Did I say that right, Kathryn?"

"Perfectly, kiddo. Before you know it, you're going to be as American as apple pie. Keep practicing in those shoes or you're going to fall flat on your ass. Maybe you should tape up your ankles or something."

"Can one of you hand me a secure cell phone?

I want to call Mitch to tell him I'll be there by six-thirty."

Isabelle handed Julia the cell phone from her pocket. Julia dialed knowing Mitch wouldn't be able to trace the call. She crossed her fingers that he wouldn't answer so she could just leave a message. She wasn't that lucky, Mitch picked up on the first ring.

"Julia, is that you?"

"Yes, Mitch, it's me. I'm just calling . . ."

Mitch interrupted her before she could say anything else. "Jesus, Julia, I am so sorry about last night. I don't know what the hell got into me. Listen, honey, I'll make it up to you. I swear I will. I promise. Are you all right? Please say you forgive me. What the hell happened to that FBI guy? Did you smooth things over? They aren't going to show up and cause a scene tonight, are they?"

"No, Mitch, I'm not all right. You cracked my ribs. I'm all taped up. There are no plans in my immediate future to forgive you. I just called to tell you I'll be at the armory around six-thirty. Give or take a few minutes either way. I don't plan on staying long but I will make an appearance. As to the agent from the FBI, I don't know his plans as he didn't confide in me. Do the wise thing, Mitch, and back out now."

"Back away from the vice presidency of the United States? Are you out of your mind. I've lusted for this my whole life and you want me to withdraw my name. The answer is, no. Crawford is old, he could bite the dust in a year or so and I'll be ready to step into his shoes. Are you on painkillers to make you say such a thing?"

"Yeah, I'm on painkillers," Julia said, clicking off the phone.

Julia looked around the room. "OK, girls, my husband is fair game tonight! Anything goes."

"Oooh, I love it when you talk like that." Kathryn laughed.

"We're all going in different limos, right? That didn't change, did it?"

Kathryn shook her head. "Nope. We're each responsible for our own gear for this little caper. Murphy stays behind tonight. Charles and Myra are coming back here so they'll take care of him till we get home. I think we're ready to roll as soon as Alexis finishes up with Julia and does her Diana Ross thing."

"She's done," Alexis said softly. "Turn around Julia."

"Julia, you look . . . beautiful!" Yoko said, running over to the dresser for a hand mirror. "You will outshine every woman at the party." This last was said so sincerely, Julia smiled and allowed herself to be hugged . . . very gently.

"Just don"t go shaking your head too much or the hair strands will come loose. And, whatever you do, don't stand under any bright lights.

Your gown is padded in all the right places. Try not to move around a lot. We'll all be within eye distance and earshot so if you want something just tug on your earlobe or something." Alexis dropped to her knees and reached for Julia's hands. "All I did was improve on something that was almost perfect to begin with. You're a beautiful woman, Julia. I want you to believe that."

"And miracles happen every day. I overheard Charles telling Myra there's a special place in Switzerland he wants to send you to. He said they work miracles for AIDS patients. Act surprised when he tells you, OK?" Kathryn whispered.

They all looked away at the hope in Julia's eyes.

"Mum's the word, girls. Dress up time!" Julia said. "We leave in exactly forty-five minutes." She pointed to her satchel and medical bag sitting next to five heavily loaded backpacks that contained the tools of their new trade. Alexis's Red Bag of tricks would be piled on top for Charles to carry down when the limousines arrived.

The wind knocked out of him, Jack stared up at the two men towering over him. They were his height, his weight. He could probably take on one of them but not two. His gaze swivelled to Mark who looked like he was going to get sick at any minute. It was a wise man who knew when to fold and walk away. No one ever said he was a wise man. "What in the damn hell . . ."

"Shut up, Emery. You talk when we say you can talk. One more peep out of you and you'll be swallowing your teeth. Agent Lane, tell this pissant who we are and where our authority comes from."

Mark wiped at the sweat forming on his brow. "Jack, each year of the presidency, according to the instructions at the FBI Academy, the president forms a small task force, for want of a better term. It usually consists of two, sometimes three men. They only answer to the president himself. They've got carte blanche. That means they can snuff us out, walk away and nothing will ever happen to them. Are you following me here, Jack?"

Jack nodded.

"When you asked me to help you, I thought it was some kind of local stuff and I was just doing a favor for a friend. But this ain't some kind of local stuff, Jack. These guys work with MI6, Interpol and all that heavy duty spy stuff that goes on all over the world, stuff we never get to hear about. Right now, I just want to forget I ever knew you. I like my job and I want to keep it. You're bush league, these guys are the big league."

Jack blinked but he didn't say anything as he struggled to an upright position. In his life he'd never seen colder or deadlier eyes. What the fuck was going on? What did he stumble onto? More to the point, where did Nikki and Myra fit into this whole damn scenario?

"You can talk now, Mr. Emery," one of the men said.

"That's Assistant District Attorney Emery to you . . . *sir.*"

"That still makes you a pissant. Now, tell us what you've been up to and why you're harassing those nice folks out there in Virginia."

Jack's mind raced. Common sense told him to opt for the truth. He told them in as straightforward a manner as he could. "I'm in law enforcement, I'm not paid to look the other way. Yes, I trespassed on Myra Rutledge's property. But it was on my own time. I was trying to get enough evidence to do something about the Marie Llewellyn case and in the course of my search, I discovered those women who congregate out there are up to something else. I think they're taking the law into their own hands. Vigilantes." He felt silly as hell and he could see that the special gold shield guys weren't buying his story.

"Mark has nothing to do with any of this," he went on. "I asked him for a favor and he helped me out. You want to cut off my dick, go ahead, but leave him out of it."

The men looked at one another. The first one shrugged. The second one smirked as he hauled Jack to his feet. "We're going to be on

199

you like white on rice from here on in, Emery. You get within a mile of those people at Pinewood and you'll never be seen or heard from again. Remember, we answer to only one man. Right now that man doesn't like you very much."

Jack saw the fist coming but couldn't duck in time. At some point during the beating, he blacked out. When he finally came to, the gold shields were gone and Mark was bending over him, his face furious because he hadn't been able to help his friend. There was blood everywhere. He picked up the phone to call 911.

"No!" Jack croaked. "Help me up and out to my car. Then you can forget you ever met me."

"Jesus, Jack, what the hell did you stumble on to? Let me patch you up first. You should go to the hospital."

"No," Jack croaked again. "Get me some aspirin and a couple of shots of whiskey. Were you telling me the truth about those guys? The president really has a goon squad? Damn, what would the American people think if they knew that?"

"Jack, leave it alone for God's sake. Don't move till I get back."

In less than a minute, Mark dropped to the floor, and opened his first aid kit and cleaned up Jack's face the best he could. "How are your ribs? Listen, Jack, I didn't mean all that shit I was spouting before."

"Yes, you did. Don't apologize. They got me

in the gut and my kidneys. I won't be able to have sex ever again. Where's the damn aspirin?"

"Here," Mark said, holding out the bottle. "I'll get the whiskey. I don't think you're supposed to take aspirin with whiskey, Jack."

"Sez who? Help me up."

"I can drive you home, Jack, and have a friend drop off your car tomorrow. Oh, shit, you aren't going home, are you?"

"No, Mark, I'm not going home. You don't need to know where I'm going. Look, I'm sorry I got you involved. I won't call you again. Take my number off your speed dial and don't bother to send me a Christmas card. I'll see you around."

Mark looked and felt like he was going to cry. "Listen, you crazy son of a bitch, you're going to get yourself killed. How am I supposed to live with that?"

"By pretending you never met me, that's how."

Agent Lane's eyes burned when the door closed behind his friend.

Ten

It could have been the Academy Awards with the glittering outfits, limousines, and hoards of reporters instead of a political turnout. The only thing missing was the red carpet and Joan Rivers. A light rain was falling when the parade of limousines from Pinewood drew up to the armory. The time was ten minutes past six when Myra Rutledge and Charles Martin exited the lead limo. The chauffeur held a huge golf umbrella over them as they scurried to the entrance, their invitation in hand.

The others followed within fifteen minutes of each other. Julia was last to arrive. Her husband was waiting inside the doorway to guide her into the vast area filled with orchids and every flower and green plant known to man. Colorful balloons were tied to the rafters and to the backs of chairs to add to the festivities. There was even an ice sculpture of the American flag on the buffet table. Julia thought it matched the one on her husband's ass except his was in living color. She said so, sotto voce.

Having lived in Washington all her life she could pick out the Secret Service, the FBI and all the other security. She mentioned that, too. Tonight, though, they were equal. She, too, wore the tiny microphone on the sleeve of her gown. All she had to do was pretend she was touching her nose and speak into the gizmo on her wrist, just the way all the security spooks did. Even the little buttons in their ears were so high-tech they couldn't be detected. The sound was short of phenomenal, allowing them to hear a whisper from ten feet away.

Mitch ignored his wife's barbed comments. "Baby, you look sensational." He looked around at the other women in the room. He appeared stunned for a moment. His wife was the best-looking woman in the entire room. She seemed to have picked up several pounds and in all the right places.

"Don't call me baby, Mitch. Save that kind of talk for your bimbos. I heard on the way here that the press is set to leak more info on you in the *Post* tomorrow. Back out now before it's too late." Her voice was colder than ice. Mitch opted not to notice.

"That's all garbage. It's politics at their worst. But, if I ever find out it was you who is doing the leaking, you'll regret it."

"Is that a threat, Mitch? If so, you might want to retract those words right now. By the way, I'm leaving you. Excuse me, I have to circulate. That's why I'm here, isn't it? Don't even think about touching me or I might scream in pain with my cracked ribs. And, by the way, the leak in tomorrow's *Post* is about that phony background story you made up on your life because you were ashamed of your own family." She shivered inwardly knowing Mitch's eyes were boring into her back.

Julia started to gingerly make her way across the vast room only to see Isabelle and Alexis at her side to run interference as they jostled their way toward the buffet table.

"There's more security here than guests. I can spot those spooks a mile away," Julia murmured. "Have you seen the Monarch family?"

"Not yet," Isabelle said.

"Good God, Alexis, you really do look like Diana Ross, right down to that wild hair. From some of the looks you're getting, I think the guests think so, too," Julia said.

"Well, that makes my day. The flowers are beautiful. Where in the hell did Yoko get all those wild orchids? By the way, where is she?"

A roving waiter appeared with a tray balanced on one hand filled with plastic flutes of champagne. The women each accepted a glass and pretended to drink. No more than a few sips, Charles had warned. You need your wits about you tonight with all the security.

"Myra is to initiate contact with the Monarchs and then she'll introduce them to Yoko. That's when it's all going to come together. I saw Nikki a moment ago and I know she's on the lookout for Jack Emery. I hate parties like this," Alexis grumbled. "Ah, we made it to the buffet. Some big bucks went into this spread," she said, smacking her lips.

Music could be heard from a small combo. Typical "oldies" fare which meant warbling by Sinatra, Crosby and Como for the older crowd. The crowd with the open checkbooks. The acoustics were horrendous. Isabelle moved off to chase down Kathryn who was talking to a fat lobbyist ogling her bosom. Alexis guided Julia to a less congested area on the far side of the buffet.

"Here comes my husband," Julia told Alexis. "Stay as close as you can. Pretend you're eating or eat, just don't leave me alone with him."

"There you are, darling," Mitch said. "Come, I want you to meet Mrs. Crawford."

"Later, Mitch."

The senator clamped his lips shut but somehow managed to say the words, "Now, Julia."

Julia ignored him. "Oh, look, there's Myra

Rutledge. Now Mitch, that's someone you want to meet. She has a war chest that just oozes money. Excuse me, I see our hospital administrator. I have to say hello. We have the whole evening ahead of us," she called over her shoulder as she moved away, Alexis behind her. The senator was left with no other recourse but to smile and reach for a plate.

"You did good, Julia. Your husband is sweating up a storm. I caught a glimpse of Governor Crawford and he does not look like a happy man. Do you suppose he's heard about the next leak?" Alexis whispered as they continued their trek through the crowds.

"Looks that way to me, too."

"Mrs. Crawford looks pretty young to me," Alexis said.

"They're all young," Julia said, sadness ringing in her voice. "They look good in photo ops. It's a trade-off. They like the prestige, the glamour of the White House and all the crap that goes with it. They lunch with their friends, grouse about their *old* husbands and have little flings on the side. They never think they'll get caught. The first Mrs. Crawford was a lovely woman, but she was plain, and she wouldn't allow them to *fix her up*. If I remember correctly, her home in Maryland was known for the rosebushes she planted. She was active in PTA. A Mom. She was a real mom until they used her up and the governor found the present Mrs.

Crawford. Everyone in this room has a story and none of them are family reading."

Towering at six feet, the Diana Ross look-alike surveyed the crowd. "Kathryn looks stunning. Do you think she'll ever fall in love again? She took her husband's death so hard," Alexis said, hoping to wipe the sadness from Julia's eyes.

"I certainly hope so. She's too young to go through life alone. I can't see Yoko or the Monarchs. Help me out here, Alexis. Do you see them?"

Frank Sinatra was warbling about a summer wind as the women finally approached Yoko who was chatting it up with a female congresswoman from Virginia. As they approached they could hear that the discussion was about orchids. Julia smiled at the congresswoman as Alexis steered Yoko out of earshot. "Have you seen those creeps?"

"If you mean the Monarchs, no. Myra was supposed to corner them and steer us in their direction. Maybe they decided not to attend. Is Julia all right?"

"Julia is holding up just fine but her husband is trying to put the squeeze on her. However, she isn't biting. She's one tough lady. The Monarchs are here, we just haven't seen them yet. You doing OK?"

"My feet are killing me. People keep staring at me."

"Suck up the pain, my friend, and people are looking at you because you're a knock-out. Head for the buffet while I try to corner Myra and Charles. Have you seen Nikki?"

"A few minutes ago. She didn't say so but I think she's on the lookout for Jack Emery. Look, there she is! Over by the middle EXIT door."

"OK, see you later. Eat something, Yoko, you're going to need your strength for what's to come later."

"Is the food any good?" Yoko queried.

"No. Yes. I don't know. I ate a shrimp. Tasted like shrimp. I want to talk to Nikki. Don't look right now but I see Myra at three o'clock and she's talking to three people who can only be the Monarchs. Give them ten minutes before you make contact, and don't forget to eat."

"Yes, Mama." Yoko giggled just as an announcement blasted through the armory via a man in a tuxedo with a microphone in hand on stage. The huge room quieted almost immediately as the governor of Maryland, the Democratic candidate for the presidency of the United States, hopped on stage followed by Mitchell Webster.

Nikki whirled around, a crumpled note in her hand. Should she stay or should she go outside? Her stomach tightened into a knot. Charles said everything had been taken care of, and yet, here was Jack sending her notes right under the eyes of the FBI, the Secret Service and God knew who else. The decision was taken out of her hands when she grew light-headed. She needed air, not this canned stuff she was breathing in great gulps. She elbowed the door and stepped outside, but didn't release her hold on the door. It was an EXIT only door. If it closed, she'd have to walk all the way around to the front.

She saw him hobble toward her holding a lopsided umbrella. In the dim yellow light over the EXIT door she could clearly see Jack's battered, bloody face. Her heart thumped in her chest. He looked to be in excruciating pain. She wanted to run to him, to say something, but she couldn't move. He stopped two feet away.

"I just wanted you to see what they did to me. Take a good look, Nik. This is all your doing. They said they'd kill me if I didn't drop my investigation. Who are *they*? Well, dear Nikki, let me tell you who *they* are. The president's goon squad sicced on me by your very own Charles Martin and Myra. They probably will kill me. You live with that because no way in hell am I going to knowingly allow all of you to break the law. You used to be a lawyer. You swore to uphold the law like I did. Now you can go back in there with all your high powered rich friends. And when they do kill me, you damn well better not show up at my funeral."

Tears rolled down Nikki's cheeks. "Jack, wait . . ."

Jack stopped, the lopsided umbrella tilted so

that it covered his knees. "Go to hell, Nicole and don't make any stops on the way down." He let go of the umbrella and it slid across the parking lot. He didn't seem to notice.

Nikki did her best to digest what she'd just seen and heard. She was in a far-away place when she felt a hand on her arm and a voice said, "Ma'am, these doors have to be closed at all times." The strong hand drew her back inside and she didn't protest. She no longer felt light-headed, just sick to her stomach. She had to find Charles and she had to find him right now.

She was startled to hear a loud voice from the stage followed by loud applause. That had to mean Senator Webster was still going to be Governor Crawford's running mate in the election in November. She swivelled in every direction to see where Myra and Charles were. How stupid she was. She moved her arm so that her wrist grazed her lips and said. "Charles, I need to see you *right now*. I'm by the middle EXIT door."

Nikki felt blind with rage when she recalled Jack's battered face, his lips split, top and bottom, his eyes swollen shut, blood oozing from all his cuts and bruises and the fact that he could barely walk. Rage was too kind of a word. What goons was he talking about? And what did he mean about someone coming back to kill him? *You swore to uphold the law like I did. And when they do kill me, you damn well better not show up at my funeral. Go to hell, Nicole, and don't make any stops on the way down.* No, no, that wasn't going to happen. She didn't sign on for anything like this.

Nikki looked away for a moment and when she looked back at the crowded room, Charles was less that a foot away from her. Right at that moment she hated the man, hated that they were all here, hated what was going to happen. She didn't know if she hated Myra and the others or not. Probably.

Charles held out his hand and Nikki shoved the crumpled note into his hand as she gave it a hard shake. "What did your . . . your goons do to Jack? He's half dead. He said they were going to kill him. He should be in a hospital. He was just doing his damn job, Charles. We could have worked around him, outwitted him. What did you do, Charles?"

"Nothing, Nikki. I made some calls. That's all I did. Let's move away from here so we can't be overheard. It was supposed to be a cease and desist, fear of God scare. I certainly didn't authorize any . . . any physical harm to his person."

"That's not good enough for me, Charles. You didn't see Jack, I did. For all I know he could have internal injuries. Look at my feet, Charles. Right now they are rooted to the floor. I'm staying right here until you come back to me with an answer that I can live with. Otherwise, I'm walking out of here and I'll never set foot in Pinewood again. I'll leave it up to you to explain to Myra and the others."

"Wait here, Nikki. This may take a little while. I'll find out what happened. Please, give me the chance to find out. Will you at least do that?"

"Yes. I'll wait right here."

A little while turned into forty-seven minutes. When Nikki saw him making his way toward her she could see the fury in his eyes. Her own eyes narrowed as she waited for an explanation.

"I'm sorry, Nikki. The orders were miscon-strued by the president's men. What happened had nothing to do with . . . with our little . . . mission. Jack's pal, the FBI agent, somehow stum-bled on to me. He called a fellow agent at Interpol who then notified MI6 that my new identity and location were about to be compro-mised. If that were to happen, I'd be whisked away in the blink of an eye and I'd never see Myra or any of you again. That's what this is all about and it has nothing to do with the Sister-hood. You're right, we can out-think and outwit Jack. Actually, I view it as a challenge."

It all rang true to Nikki's ears. She found her-self nodding. "I want your personal word that Jack is safe from physical harm, Charles."

"You have it, Nikki. I know how much you love him." Nikki didn't bother to deny it this time around. "I can send over medical help if you like, to his apartment."

"Yes, do that, Charles," Nikki said flatly. "What's going on?"

"Myra is entertaining the Monarch family. They're hanging on her every word. When Myra said she could possibly arrange an ambassadorship, all three of them literally swooned. Myra was getting ready to introduce them to Yoko when you flashed me. Is there anything else, Nikki?"

Nikki shook her head before she made her way through the crowd of people, her thoughts not on the mission ahead of them but on Jack Emery.

Eleven

Myra Rutledge wore a smile that made her face ache. This Monarch family was despicable and yet here she was talking to them and making them phony promises. All they did, the three of them, was feed off innocent people who bought into their HMOs so their families could be protected in case of illness. Three vultures waiting to pounce on the innocent.

She really had to stop smiling; her teeth were starting to ache. Her eyes left the little group for a few seconds as she tried to locate the girls. Where was Yoko? Ah, there she was, headed her way. A sigh escaped her lips.

Myra was resplendent in diamonds and designer wear, far above what Elaine Monarch strived to be. If she had to take a wild guess, the Monarchs' glittering attire probably cost somewhere in the neighborhood of fifty thousand, give or take a few thousand dollars, and they still looked tacky and artificial. She noticed early on that no one at the event made any effort to either shake their hands or even speak with them unless they initiated the contact. HMO was truly a dirty set of initials in this fair city.

Elaine Monarch reached for Myra's arm. "You do understand that my husband and I would be more than willing *to pay* for the ambassadorship. We don't even care what country it is."

Myra pretended horror. At least she could stop smiling for a few minutes. "No, dear lady. One does not pay for such a position. They pay you. One just accepts graciously when one is appointed. I have considerable influence and will certainly put in a kind word on your behalf. I don't see any harm in making a donation to some worthy cause if you're successful in being appointed." *Dear God, please don't let me gag.*

"You are so very kind, Mrs. Rutledge. Isn't she kind, Derek? We almost didn't come this evening but Ethan said we needed to show our support for the Democrats. Meeting you, Mrs. Rutledge, has been the highlight of the evening," Elaine continued to gush.

Myra had to smile again. "I so enjoyed hearing about your . . . ah, various collections. You did say you have many priceless antiquities of Ming origin, didn't you?'

The skinny dandy son named Ethan chirped up. "Mother has a fabulous collection and is constantly on the lookout for more. They're incredibly hard to come by as I'm sure you know. Are you a collector, Mrs. Rutledge?'

"Of many things, young man." She could tell by the look in Ethan's eyes that Yoko was close by. He did everything but drool, as did his pudgy, balding father. Elaine's head went a little higher, her see-through hair glistening in the artificial light.

Yoko's voice when she spoke was soft, cultured and *whispery*. "I wonder if I might have a quiet word with you, Mrs. Rutledge, before I leave?"

"But of course, my dear. Let me introduce you to this delightful little family. Elaine and Derek Monarch, and their son, Ethan. This is Su Li. She is a descendent of the Ming dynasty. Isn't that absolutely amazing? She probably knows everything there is to know about the treasures you've been collecting." Yoko gave a slight nod of her head, her hands folded demurely in front of her. Ethan looked like his eyes were going to pop right out of his head. His father was so busy undressing Yoko with his eyes he didn't notice the jealous glare in his wife's eyes. Myra felt pleased at what she was seeing. She decided to stoke the fire a little. "Su Li will be your competition for the ambassadorship, Mrs. Monarch. She really doesn't want it, though. We've been doing some arm twisting."

"My father is old-fashioned," Yoko explained. "He does not believe women belong in the political arena but I am a modern Chinese. It's just that my life is so very full right now that I have no time to take on such a prestigious position and do it justice. Still, if the powers that be offer it to me, I would want to do my duty and would probably accept the appointment," she said sweetly. Elaine Monarch scowled at these words.

Myra smiled again. "Su is being modest. She single-handedly runs her father's import-export business. Perhaps you've heard of it, Li Luc Imports."

Derek Monarch's eyebrows shot upward as did his son's. "Your father owns Li Luc Imports?"

"Yes," Yoko said quietly.

Obviously, Myra thought, the male members of the Monarch family were aware of Li Luc Imports's financial status. She could tell they were impressed by their greedy expressions. Elaine had no clue what anyone was talking about. Myra looked around, trying not to be obvious about it. The crowd of supporters was starting to thin out. The buffet table was a mess, the way buffet tables always were at the end of a party. The musicians were packing up their equipment. Where were the girls?

"The night's still young," Derek Monarch said

as he looked down at his watch. We live in Manassas which isn't far from here. Would you ladies like to come up with us so we can show you our treasures and perhaps talk a little about that ambassadorship?"

Yoko tilted her head sideways. "I am so sorry but I cannot make it this evening. I am leaving for China early in the morning. It was a pleasure meeting you all." She bowed slightly.

Elaine's see-through hair waved in the breeze created by the various fans overhead. "So, does that mean you do or do not want to be appointed to the ambassadorship. Miss Li?"

Yoko lowered her gaze. "The appointment has not been offered to me as yet, Madam Monarch. Mrs. Rutledge, I understand, will have considerable input when it is time to make the final decision. She is aware of my position. Good night, everyone, it was a pleasure to meet you all."

"Can I escort you to your car?" Ethan asked.

"That would be very kind of you, Mr. Monarch." As they walked away, Myra could hear Yoko ask, "And what is it you do, sir?"

Myra eyed the offensive woman standing in front of her. She knew both husband and wife would kiss her feet if she asked them to. She held out her hand when she saw Isabelle waving across the room. Elaine Monarch looked like she wanted to cry. She poked her husband on the arm. He turned to Myra and said, "We'd be honored if you could see your way to joining us in a nightcap somewhere in the city, Mrs. Rutledge, if you aren't up to a trip to Manassas."

"There's nothing I would like more than that, Mr. Monarch. Unfortunately, I have house guests at home. Perhaps another time. If you're amenable, Mrs. Monarch, and if my schedule permits, we could do lunch next week. By then I should have more information on the ambassadorship."

The relief on Elaine's face was short of comic. "Derek, give Mrs. Rutledge one of your business cards. I'll wait for your call. I have the entire week free, dear lady."

I just bet you do. Myra's teeth were starting to ache again as she forced still another smile. It was a relief to shake hands and move away.

As Myra made her way to the front exit, stopping to chat with a federal judge here, a socialite there and a handful of other dignitaries she could hardly wait to get in the car and get home so she could take a shower. All she could think about was the obnoxious Monarch family and how they'd fleeced their subscribers to satisfy their own greed.

Outside, the rain came down in torrents as limo drivers jockeyed for position fearing their customers' wrath at not being by the door to greet them. Security was sloppy at best.

Charles appeared as if by magic holding a large black umbrella. Myra stepped under it. She squeezed Charles's arm. All around her people were muttering and some were cursing the weather, the security and the limo drivers. "I suggest we walk down the road to where our car waits. That's if you don't mind getting wet."

"You can keep me warm, darling." Myra's eyes twinkled. "Let's hurry, though, before those three vultures come anywhere close. As it is, I can't wait to take a shower."

"Were they that bad, Myra?"

"Worse, Charles. All I could think about was all the people who were denied coverage with deadly consequences. Can you imagine people like that coveting an ambassadorship?"

"Yes, dear, I can imagine it. Look, Myra, there's Kathryn with her truck backed up to the back of the armory. And, there's Yoko! They look like our girls. It's amazing how glamorous they can look one minute and the next they're just our girls."

Myra did her best to peer into the driving rain. She saw two figures running back and forth with flowers and plants in their hands. Whistles shrilled and blasted as the local police tried to direct traffic in the soggy night.

Twenty minutes passed before Charles looked down at his digital watch that glowed blue in the dark. "On the count of five, we should have total darkness. One, two, three, four, five!" Myra clutched his arm as the world turned totally dark. "Three minutes before our man drives the Monarch Town Car right up the ramp into

Kathryn's truck. Another minute to discard the ramp and Kathryn will take off. The girls are right behind the rig in their individual limousines. No one will ever be the wiser. The only thing the security detail is concerned with at this moment is the governor."

"Darling, you are too clever. I'm not even going to ask you how you arranged all of this."

"We arranged the cars just as Yoko left. It wasn't easy with all the security, and a limousine is not the easiest vehicle to back up and turn around. I relied on the congestion, everyone's short temper and, of course, this pouring rain which worked to our advantage."

"What about Julia and her husband. Don't they have a security detail?"

"They *did* have a security detail. Julia pulled off what Kathryn would call the old switcheroo. The detail is following an eighty-year-old couple from Arlington. All of our people, as I speak, are on their way to Manassas. We can now go home knowing the Monarch family and Senator Webster are in capable hands." Charles looked at his watch again as he counted under his breath. "Three minutes and counting. The lamp posts will come to life and our caravan will be safely out of sight. I just love this rain, don't you, Myra?"

Myra giggled as she snuggled closer to Charles. "I do love the rain but I love you more. What are we going to do when we get home, Charles?"

PAYBACK

Charles looked at Myra in the dim yellowish light of the limo. "Unfortunately, not what we would both like to do. We have a job to do."

Myra wiggled even closer, "Oh . . . poop!"

Twelve

Jack Emery did his best to bellow, "Come in" to the person knocking on his door. It came out little better than a hoarse croak. He flopped back on the sofa, drained with the effort. *They* were probably coming back to finish the job they started. He wondered what it would feel like to die, to take his last breath, to see the world turn fuzzy and gray. Would he see the white light, the angels everyone talked about, when he drew his last breath?

He tried to open his eyes but finally gave up. "Just fucking do it and get it over with. I'm an easy target, I can't move. Well, what the hell are you waiting for? Look, my eyes are closed. Shoot me and get it over with."

"Jack, it's me, Mark. Look, I'm sorry the way all that crap went down back at my place. I came over to take you to the hospital. You need some help, buddy. For whatever it's worth, I'm on your side. I admit, back there, they scared the living crap out of me. Then I realized I can't stand still for that kind of thing just the way you can't. I'd rather quit. After I get you patched up, I'm calling my boss and whatever happens, happens. Worst case scenario, we open up our own security agency. I have some money saved. My dad will lend me the rest to get us up on our feet."

"Are you nuts! You're looking at a real loser here. Why in the hell would you want to tie yourself up with someone like me? Forget it. Go home. Forget you ever knew me. Let me lie here and die. Go on, get out of here, Mark."

Mark ignored the tortured words as he headed for the kitchen and the freezer. He took out a plastic bag of peas and shook them loose. Jack had to be the only single guy in the world who kept frozen peas in his freezer. He walked back to his friend and placed the package on his battered face. He then made his way to the bathroom and rummaged till he found a first aid kit. He was on his knees about to dress some of Jack's cuts when a knock sounded at the door. In a heartbeat, he was on his feet, his gun in his hand. "Come in." The sound of the hammer clicking back was so loud in the quiet room, Jack almost fainted.

A middle-aged woman dressed in a nurse's uniform and a swarthy man wearing a white lab coat and carrying a medical bag stepped into the room. They seemed oblivious to the drawn gun. "You won't need the gun, young man. We're here to help Mr. Emery and to offer . . . apologies." At least that's what Jack thought he said, his accent heavy and guttural.

"I don't think so," Mark said. "How do we know you aren't here to finish the job? No shots. No nothing. Turn around and leave. I'll take care of my friend."

"No. Your president sends his sincere regrets for this unfortunate turn of events. Allow us to help make it right," the guttural voice said.

Mark dropped to a crouch to shield Jack but not before he stiff-armed the nurse. "We don't need your help. I'll take care of my friend."

Jack would have cried if he could have made his tear ducts work. Loyalty was something he hadn't encountered in a long time. He continued to listen to his friend.

"You are to call this number," the guttural voice said, handing over a slip of paper.

"Yeah, like I'm really going to do that and lay down my gun, too. Take a hike, buddy. There's no way you're squirting anything into my friend's veins."

"Call the number, Mark, or hand me the phone and I'll do it," Jack said. "Tell them to back off toward the door."

"You heard the man," Mark said, brandishing the gun. Both white-coated figures moved backward while Jack dialed the number Mark read from the slip of paper in his free hand.

"United States White House."

Jack ended the call. "It was the White House. What now, Coach. I'm in a lot of pain, here, buddy."

"OK, open the bag and let's see what you got. You can examine him while I watch. No shots, no pills. Clean him up and dress the cuts. That's it. *Capice!*"

An hour later when Jack was done howling and kicking his feet, the doctor stepped backward. "Give him these every four hours for pain. It's Demerol. The word is written on the tablet. They're safe. I taped his ribs. He should see his own doctor as soon as he's comfortable doing so. If his condition changes, you can call me at this number," the doctor said, scribbling a cell phone number on the corner of a magazine on the coffee table. "The number is only good for twenty-four hours at which point it will be disconnected. The best thing for him right now is sleep. We can see ourselves out."

Mark stayed a safe distance behind the couple as they exited the apartment. He shot the dead bolt and the other two locks Jack had personally installed. He himself had the same kind of locks at his own apartment. No sense looking for more trouble.

"Guess they belong to the spook brigade," Jack mumbled. "Get me some whiskey, Mark. It's in the kitchen cabinet. I went to the armory, Mark."

"Tell me something I don't already know," Mark said, looking around the messy apartment. "You really should clean this place up, Jack. You could probably catch a disease just living here."

"Yeah, yeah, yeah. I kind of lost all heart when Nikki dumped me. I always kept it clean for her. The whiskey, Mark?"

Mark poured liberally and then had second thoughts so he watered down the Jim Beam. Jack swallowed it in two gulps.

Mark stuffed the gun he was still holding into the shoulder holster under his armpit. He perched on the end of the couch. "What do you want me to do, Jack?"

Jack knew he was about to fade out. "I don't know, Mark. You know as much as I do right now. Hell, man, you're FBI. If this was your case and there were no obstacles, what would you do? Treat it like it's the most important case on your desk and go on from there. You can use my computer. My password is . . . is . . . Nikki. Don't let me sleep too long, OK?"

"Yeah, sure, Jack."

Mark looked around. If there was one thing he couldn't stand, it was a mess. One of seven children, he'd been taught at an early age how to clean, cook, do laundry, and take care of himself. He started to work. First, he cleared out all the trash, empty pizza boxes, empty Chinese containers and stacks and stacks of beer bottles. The empty dishwasher yawned in his face. He loaded it and what didn't fit, he soaked in the double kitchen sink. He used the vacuum and Dust Buster and loaded the washing machine with a load of pitiful-looking towels. The dirty clothes strewn all over the floor went into an already overstuffed hamper.

Now, he could sit down at the computer where he tapped away for hours without taking a break. When he finally looked up he was surprised to see gray light seeping through the open blinds. It was still raining.

Mark checked on Jack and then went into the kitchen to make coffee and toast for himself. He massaged his neck and shoulders as his mind raced. The big question in his mind was what seven very diverse women had in common? Add one very important man named Charles Martin to the mix and what did he have?

One big mother of a mess was the answer.

Well, hell, he was a computer programmer for the FBI. Even the CIA and the DOJ borrowed him from time to time because he was beyond good. How modest he was, he thought. In the spook world he traveled in, you had to blow your own horn from time to time. He'd installed

and programmed some of the most sophisticated computers in all three organizations. As
such, he knew where the fire walls and back doors
were, how to undo and patch up the fire walls so
no one would notice if he accessed them. The
big question was, did he really want to put his
ass on the line for Jack Emery?

Coffee cup in hand, Mark made his way back
to Jack's computer. He stopped a moment to
stare down at his sleeping friend. The answer
was yes.

Thirteen

Julia Webster leaned back against the plush cushions of the limousine. She was exhausted but she'd done her part. The driver of the limousine she and Mitch were riding in would have Kathryn's rig in sight all the way to Manassas, Virginia. For now she just had to listen to her husband's tirade which was getting louder by the moment. It was typical Mitch. Place blame, cry poor poor me. If she wanted to, she could recite the litany verbatim.

"Where the hell are we going?" Mitch bellowed. "This isn't the way to Georgetown! Where's our detail? You really are stupid, Julia. We're in the wrong limousine! This is your fault.

Where the hell are we going?" he bellowed a second time.

Julia yawned elaborately. "You're right, we're in the wrong limousine. Your detail is following some Republican couple to Arlington. Or maybe it's Alexandria. We're going to Manassas to have drinks with those horrid Monarch HMO people. I'd appreciate it if you'd lower your voice. You're giving me a headache."

Not about to give up, Mitch moved forward until he was next to the partition separating the driver from the passengers. "Turn this damn car around and take me home. To Georgetown. We changed our mind, we don't want to go to Manassas."

"Too late, sir," came the response. Isabelle took her eyes off the road for a minute to glare at her passenger. "Sit down and buckle your seat belt. If you force me to stop this car, you won't like the consequences."

"Are you threatening me?" Mitch shouted.

"Yes," Isabelle shouted in return.

"Do you know who I am, driver? I'm a United States senator! You just threatened a United States senator! I can have you thrown in jail for threatening me."

"Go for it, Senator!" Isabelle snapped.

Julia smiled to herself. Her eyes still closed, she sensed Mitch returning to his seat. She knew he was searching for his cell phone he'd laid on the seat earlier. She was now sitting on it. She smiled again.

"Well, we'll just see about this. Where's my cell phone, Julia?"

"I have no idea, Mitchell. Maybe you left it back at the armory."

"I brought it with me. Will you move, please. Maybe it slid across the seat."

Julia made a pretense of looking and patting the seat. "No, Mitchell, it isn't here."

"Then let me use yours. C'mon, c'mon. I think we're being hijacked here. Though who would be stupid enough to do something like that boggles my mind."

Julia handed over her evening purse. "There was no room for a cell phone so I left it in my car. Relax, Mitchell, and think about how you can snooker the Monarchs into doing some fund-raising for your campaign. The night's still young. We'll be back home by midnight."

"What was that crap before about leaving me? You said if I gave you that list you'd stand by me."

"I lied."

"Oh, no, it doesn't work that way. I need you, Julia. We're going to discuss this when we get back home."

"Whatever you say, Mitchell." Like that was really going to happen.

Fifteen minutes later the limousine slowed to a crawl.

Up ahead, Kathryn's eighteen-wheeler approached the security panel outside the Monarch estate. Kathryn glared into the electric eye and speaking box. She pressed a series of numbers on a portable keypad Charles had given her. The gates—some kind of thick wood mixed with heavy iron—swung open. The only thing missing was coiled razor wire. Kathryn pulled ahead and then waited until Isabelle's limousine cleared the gates before she pressed a second series of numbers. She waited another few minutes until she was certain the gates were closed and locked. She then pressed a third set of numbers that jammed the gates. Safe.

Nikki was in the passenger seat while Yoko was settled in the small area where Kathryn slept when she was on the road. In the back of the truck, the Monarch family huddled together inside their car in the dark. Alexis was their driver.

"Do you suppose the Monarchs think all this security makes them important or do they have something inside they don't want anyone to see? They aren't the type to hide out. They like to be seen. It is impressive, though. I wonder how many of their subscribers had to die for them to get all of this," Nikki said.

"Too many," Kathryn said curtly. "Nikki, call Charles and tell him we're inside the gates."

The driveway that looked more like a two

lane highway was lined with tall cypress trees that formed a canopy as the big truck lumbered around the snake-like road that was a mile long.

"I can't wait to see this place in the daylight. I read in one of the reports that the Monarchs pay their ground keepers two hundred thousand bucks a year! Do you believe that? This is way too decadent for me."

Kathryn drove the rig up to a concrete apron in front of an eight-car garage. She cut the engine, hopped out of the cab, and ran around to the back to unlock the huge door. She sucked in her breath when the huge metal door slid upward. Headlights glared in the darkness. With Nikki's help, she lowered the metal treads that would allow Alexis to back the Town Car out.

"You ready, Nikki?"

"Yep." Nikki pulled a nine-millimeter Glock out of the waistband of her slacks and brandished it about. "Open the door!" Kathryn obliged. Ethan Monarch was the first one out as he swung his arms ready to do battle. Kathryn brought up her elbow and smacked him square in the throat. He collapsed to his knees. He looked like he was praying as he gasped and sputtered.

Elaine Monarch was next. She looked frightened. "What do you want? We'll give you anything you want. Don't kill us. Please don't kill us."

Kathryn looked at Nikki and shrugged. She looked back at Elaine. "Clarify what you mean by, 'anything.'"

"Whatever you want," Derek said as he minced his way over to stand next to his wife.

"OK, we'll think about it. Let's go in the house. That goes for you, too, Junior," Kathryn said, giving the young man a none too gentle kick with her booted foot. "Don't even think about pressing the panic buttons on the alarm system. They've been disabled. I'll take it as an act of bad faith if you try. Move!"

"Who are you people?" Derek asked, his voice quivering with fright.

Nikki waved the Glock. The trio picked up their feet and practically scampered to a set of French doors. Nikki aimed the gun and shot off the lock. She blew imaginary smoke from the barrel of the gun. The trio moaned as they grasped at one another.

"Great shooting, girl!" Kathryn said. "Lights, people!"

Elaine scurried to a row of switches inside the door. Kathryn and Nikki both blinked. It wasn't a room, it was a cavern. They took a minute to look around in disbelief. Oriental and Aubusson rugs, inlaid marble, French parquet, stained glass skylights and windows, priceless paintings, brocade-covered furniture, spindly tables with spindly legs. Nikki looked upward at the vaulted ceiling that had cherubs and angels floating overhead. "What's this room?" Nikki asked, directing her question at Elaine.

Elaine looked like she was trying to decide if there was a right or wrong answer to the question. "It's just . . . a room. We don't use it."

"Then why do you have it?" Kathryn asked.

"To . . . to hold our treasures. We . . . we call it the French room. Everything in this room is priceless, one of a kind. Things a collector dreams about," Elaine responded. She appeared relieved that she'd apparently given the right answer.

"We sent your servants on a little vacation. The chauffeur and the garden crew, too. There's no one here but us," Nikki said as she continued looking around.

"Where is your home office? According to this," Kathryn said, pulling a folded sheet of paper out of her shirt pocket, "it's next to a suite of rooms on the second floor. Who wants to lead the way? And your home theater, where is that?" Derek pointed to the doorway on the left.

"Where's the safe?" Nikki asked.

"We don't have a safe," Derek bleated.

Kathryn waved the paper. "Rule number one. Don't lie to us. If you do, you will be punished," she singsonged. "Take us to the office. Lead the way, Junior. Mummy and Daddy, follow Junior."

Junior led the way through two more cavernous rooms—a Japanese room and a Chinese room. Kathryn and Nikki rolled their eyes at one another. The rooms were *stuffed* with treasures. "Does this remind you of a museum?" Nikki whispered.

"Yeah, one where the curator has really bad taste. Ah, we're here," Kathryn said, poking her head into the Monarchs' private office. She whistled at what she was seeing. Nikki simply gawked.

"Yo, Derek, what is all this?" Kathryn asked, waving her arms about. "Remember rule number one when you answer."

"Tell them, Derek," Elaine said, clutching her husband's arm.

"Don't tell them anything, Pop. This is a home invasion," Ethan squawked hoarsely. "You're going to pay for this," he squawked again.

Nikki waved her gun. "I-don't-think-so! Lookee here, we're the ones with the gun." Ethan clamped his lips shut.

"It's a duplicate of Monarch's home office," Derek said. "Everything is at my fingertips. Tell me why you're doing this."

"Really," Kathryn drawled. "This is Washington. You gotta keep up with the trends. I'm thinking this is a trendy operation. No more questions. Show my friend how everything ties together while your wife shows me where your home safe is. But before we do that, Junior, strip down and then sit down. Well, what are you waiting for, strip!"

"Oh, my Godddd!" Elaine dithered. Her eyes sparked momentarily as though she understood she would be next. "Is it really necessary to do this? We're cooperating with you. Why do you have to humiliate us?"

"Because we can," Kathryn said coldly. "Humiliation is the least of your worries."

Ethan stared defiantly at Nikki and the gun she was holding.

"Do you really want me to count to three?" Nikki aimed the gun and mouthed the numbers one through three. When Ethan made no move to undress, she fired at the point of his shoe. Shiny black patent leather and splinters of hardwood flew upward. And a waterfall of blood mixed with black nylon from his sock. Elaine stumbled. Kathryn didn't look back.

"Where the hell is the safe, Elaine? We've been walking for a long time here. You better not be stalling me," Kathryn hissed angrily.

"It's in the private wing of the house. We really don't use this section. It's for . . ."

"I know, housing your treasures. You should get one of those moving walkways."

"We looked into it but it didn't . . . seem feasible," Elaine whined. "This is the beginning of the private wing."

Kathryn looked around. More cavernous rooms, more priceless rugs and paintings. "OK, show me the safe and open it up."

Elaine Monarch moved toward a door in the center of what looked like a sitting room that held no less than seven ugly couches and eleven ugly armchairs. She opened the door, stepped through the opening and then opened another door. She stood to the side. Kathryn gaped at the heavy steel door. A vault similar to those used in banks. Her insides started to twitch. "Open it!"

"It can only be opened at three minutes past the hour. The time is precise." Elaine looked down at the diamond studded watch on her wrist and then at the digital clock mounted in the vault door. "We have five minutes to wait," she said nervously.

Five minutes later a tiny ping of sound could be heard from the mounted clock on the vault door. Elaine moved forward and punched in numbers. It took all her strength to turn the huge wheel but finally the door moved and then slid silently to the side on well oiled hinges. She pressed another switch that flooded the room with light.

The inside of the vault was possibly eight by ten feet in size with floor to ceiling shelves on all three walls. A small chair and metal table sat in the middle of the room. An overhead fan whirred to circulate the air. Probably so the money lining the shelves wouldn't dry out, Kathryn thought inanely.

She turned to her hostess and said, "I really don't have time to count all this but how much money is on those shelves? Remember rule number one."

"Twenty-five million dollars," Elaine mumbled.

"And the jewelry? That is jewelry in those velvet boxes, right?"

"Around sixteen million," Elaine mumbled again.

"All right, let's just leave this door open for now. Is there a shortcut back to your offices?"

"Yes."

"Then hit it, lady. Don't mess with me again. Why did you take me on the scenic route instead of the shortcut?"

"Why should I help you? You're going to kill us, aren't you? You people have no mercy."

Kathryn chewed on her lower lip. "No, we don't. Have mercy, that is. Come on, pick up those stilettos and let's move. We wasted enough time with your scenic tour." Elaine teetered on her spike heels but did as Kathryn ordered. Both women were breathless when they entered the Monarch home office.

Both senior and junior Monarch were stark naked. It wasn't a pretty sight. "You're next,

Mom," Nikki said, waving the gun. Elaine started to cry. "Don't make me help you." Elaine complied. A naked Elaine was not some kind of pretty. "OK, sit down," Nikki said, indicating three small chairs on casters as she pulled a roll of duct tape out of her back-pack and tossed it to Kathryn.

"Oh, God, why are you doing this to us? I opened the safe. Take the money and leave us alone." Elaine sobbed.

Nikki shoved her gun into the belt of her slacks the moment Kathryn secured the little family to the swivel chairs. Cell phone in hand, she called Charles but not before Kathryn whispered in her ear. "All our chicks in the area are secure. Tell me what to do." Nikki scribbled furiously. "Got it. I'll get back to you," she told Charles.

"Turn them around so they can see the monitor." Kathryn turned the chairs and waited.

"I'm only going to ask you these questions once. If you stall me, give me the wrong answers, you will feel"—she pointed to the cattle prod Kathryn was holding upright—"some severe pain. How do I access the business account?"

Derek blurted the information, his eyes never leaving the cattle prod. Ethan glared defiantly. Elaine continued to sob.

The question and answer routine went on for

twenty minutes. When Nikki had all the information she needed she nodded to Kathryn.

A picture of a small blonde girl flashed on the screen. It was followed by pictures of a middle-aged man and then an elderly lady in a white shawl. Picture after picture appeared on the screen. The Monarch family looked at each picture not understanding what they were seeing but they didn't ask any questions.

Then a series of pictures, possibly a hundred or so, appeared on the screen. They were all small children from newborns to children five or six years of age. All looked listless, their arms dangling at their sides. They looked like tiny robots.

Thirty minutes later, Nikki finally stopped popping pictures. She held up a thick stack of photos six inches thick. "Do you know who those people are?" she demanded.

"How could we possibly know that?" Elaine cried. "Just take the money and leave us alone. What are you doing? What do you want from us?"

"We're going to give all your money away. To people like those you just saw on the screen. And, to these," Nikki said, wagging the stack of photos in their direction. "Those people are your subscribers. You denied their claims. Most of them died because they couldn't get the care they needed. The children were all born with

Erb's Palsy because their mothers were sent to a doctor Monarch approved of. When they were born, there was no doctor in attendance, the families tried to sue Monarch. Once again, you greedy people ordered arbitration by retired judges who were on your payroll. Needless to say, the verdicts were always on Monarch's side because those judges didn't want to lose the income you provided. Someone has to pay for that. We find you guilty as charged so you are going to pay. We're going to bankrupt all three of your Monarch HMOs. And we're going to ruin all the people who have helped you launder that money sitting in the vault in your personal quarters. When we're done with you, we're going after the doctor, his staff and all those bloodsucking judges on your payroll."

Elaine continued to wail. Senior and Junior glared. They were getting good at it.

"Now, give me your personal bank information and that also includes all your off-shore accounts. Come on now, don't be shy. Kathryn you might want to . . . ah . . . prod them a little to move things along."

Kathryn yanked at the charged up cattle prod and gave Junior and Senior a none too gentle prod. They screamed in pain just as a knock sounded on the door. Elaine stomped her bare feet and tried to shout something but the duct tape Kathryn quickly put on muffled the sound.

"Oh, gee whiz, company," Nikki said as she busily clicked the keys in front of her. She nodded to Kathryn who obediently trotted across the room to open the door. Julia waltzed through, followed by her husband. Kathryn slammed and locked the door.

Mitch Webster looked around the room, the color draining from his face.

Julia walked over to the duct-taped family members, leaned over and said, "I'm a doctor. Are you all right?" Her tone clearly indicated she didn't care one way or the other. She dipped her hand into one of the pockets of her wrap and brought out a bouquet of hypodermic syringes. "You name it and I got it," she said cheerfully.

"Julia! What the hell is going on here? Who are these people?"

"Well that one and that one," Julia said, pointing to Nikki and Kathryn, "are my friends. These three are scum of the earth. Strip down, Mitch!" Julia looked at Kathryn and said, "I don't smell it, do you?" Kathryn shrugged, not understanding the question. Julia laughed. "Testosterone! I think it evaporated." She turned her attention back to her husband, the bouquet of syringes still in her hand. "Strip or you get one of each!"

"Are you crazy?"

The charged up cattle prod snapped outward

and Mitch doubled over. Kathryn struck a second and third time. Mitch took off his clothes. Kathryn clucked her tongue. "You bad boys never seem to learn."

A knock sounded on the door.

"Oh, gee whiz, more company," Nikki gurgled as she sent blizzards of numbers flying across the screen.

Kathryn tossed the roll of duct tape to Julia who shoved her husband onto the last chair in the office. "My goodness, where *are* my manners? I'd like you all to meet my philandering husband, Senator Mitchell Webster. Mitch, these lovely naked people are the Monarchs of the infamous Monarch HMOs. We're giving away all their money and making restitution to their subscribers. Actually, what we're doing is bankrupting them and their company."

Mitch opened his mouth to snarl something but Julia slapped a strip of tape over his mouth.

The door flew inward as Kathryn backed up. Two black clad figures brandishing swords danced into the room. Only their eyes were visible in the black hoods. Yoko advanced, brandishing a wicked-looking sword as she yelled, "*Eyow!*" she followed up with a high pirouette. A puff of smoke exploded from her hand before a steel star sailed through the air to land between Ethan Monarch's legs. Urine squirted high in the air.

Not to be outdone, Alexis whooped, whirled and dipped as she, too, delivered puffs of smoke and loud bloodcurdling shouts.

"Ninjas!" Derek Monarch moaned pitifully, his eyes on the star between his son's legs.

Elaine screamed at the top of her lungs.

Derek looked down at his privates and then at the swords in the hands of the black clad figures. Mitch tried to cross his legs. "Just think of us as a bunch of party animals, Mitch." Then Julia laughed. And laughed.

"By the way, we're all together," Nikki called from her computer station. "It's time to divvy up," she called out cheerfully. She pointed to Kathryn. "Do you have any special causes?"

"Let me think. Can I pick anyone I want?"

Nikki nodded.

"Let's donate twenty thousand to Greenpeace. Another twenty thousand to the Sierra Club. Two million to the ASPCA. Twenty million to Emily Sanchez's family." Kathryn turned to the Monarchs. "Monarch said the bone marrow Emily needed was unnecessary. Emily died. Nah, make that twenty-five million. I heard the Cartoon Network is in financial trouble. Let's give them a hundred thousand. Murphy loves watching cartoons."

Nikki directed her next comment to Derek Monarch. "We're sending a year's premiums back to all your subscribers and advising them to sign on with a PPO opposed to an HMO. All existing claims will be paid *in full*. We're also ignoring the deductibles."

It was Julia's turn. She looked at the robust bottom line on Nikki's chart. "Ten million to the Haggerty family. Mr. and Mrs. Haggerty used up all their savings and are currently in the welfare system because you denied the coverage that would have made him whole. Greed is a terrible thing."

Derek Monarch started to drool when he realized what was happening. Ethan slumped in his chair as his millions were allocated to worthy recipients. Elaine wept noisily, so noisily Kathryn pointed the cattle prod at her perky silicone breasts. She shut up instantly and then hiccupped.

"You raided this company for your own personal greed," Nikki said. "We simply can't allow that. We find you three, guilty as charged! Damn, I already said that, didn't I? Well, that's what we're doing."

"Oh, dear, Mitch wants to say something," Julia said, walking over to her husband. She yanked at the strip of duct tape.

"I don't know these people. If they did what they did then they deserve this but what the hell am I doing here? I hate HMOs. It's the Republicans who love those HMOs. I'm a goddamn

Democrat. I demand you let me loose immediately."

"Demand all you want, Mitch. We're going to deal with you later. Make another peep and the Ninjas can have you. Do I make myself clear?"

"Are we having fun yet?" Kathryn chortled.

"I didn't know any of this," Elaine Monarch sobbed. "I didn't know those people died. How could you do such a thing, Derek?"

"Shut up, Elaine. Where did you think the money came from for . . . all of this?"

"Your salary. That's what you told me. Oh, God, Oh, God!" She sobbed.

"Ooops, more company," Nikki said when a knock was heard at the door. The two Ninjas stepped aside as Julia ran to open it.

"Refreshments!" Isabelle trilled as she trundled in a huge dolly laden with food.

Nikki stepped away from the computer to stand in front of the four bound figures strapped to the chairs. "OK, the fun's over. Do any of you four have even one compassionate bone in your bodies? How could you knowingly withhold crucial medical care to those who need it the most? How? Do you have any idea how many deaths and crippling illnesses are lying on your personal doorstep?" She didn't expect an answer and she didn't get one.

"As of Monday morning, Monarch's doors

are closed. Every account that has your name or a family member's name on it is now carrying a zero balance. We've only made a dent in what we plan to do to right all the wrongs you three made in the name of your greed. It's going to take us weeks to notify and make restitution to all those you've damaged but it will be done. You are now going to sign off on some quit claim deeds to all the different properties you own. Everything is going to be sold and given to the people you bilked. All your cars, your boats, that fancy Gulfstream plane will go on the auction block. The whole ball of wax. But first the three of you are going to sign this power of attorney allowing me to dispose of your assets and the company's assets. Kathryn, untie their writing hands then bind them back up."

"Why am I here?" Mitch bellowed. "I'm a goddamn United States senator! I demand you release me immediately. You better not be thinking about murdering anyone!"

Isabelle, who was spreading caviar on crackers and handing them out with glasses of champagne, looked at Julia and said, "This might be a good time to tell your husband why he's here."

"I think you're right. Take the tape off one of his hands so he can read my medical report."

Kathryn, her hands shaking, undid the tape and handed him Julia's diagnosis. She stepped back to watch the senator.

"What the hell is this? It says you . . . it says you have AIDS! I knew it! I knew you were screwing around! You bitch!"

"Oh, God! Oh, God! Did you touch me?" Elaine Monarch squealed in fright.

Julia closed her eyes and would have dropped to the floor but Nikki caught her. Kathryn handed the senator a second medical report. An evil grin stretched across her face. "Read it and weep, Senator!"

"You gave me AIDS! I'll kill you for this."

Isabelle was in his face in the blink of an eye. "Look at the dates, Senator. *You* gave AIDS to your wife. You're the one. And you infected everyone you came in contact with. That's why your wife wanted the list of women you slept with. You have AIDS, Senator Webster."

"You're lying! You're all crazy! I didn't have a blood test," the senator blustered.

"You gave blood, you just don't remember. I took a blood sample while you were sleeping. I am a doctor, you know. I had you tested. I'm more than willing to leak *that* to the *Post,*" Julia said.

Mitch continued to bluster. "I don't believe you. I feel fine. I'm healthy as a horse. You're lying!"

"I felt fine, too, in the beginning. The drugs will work for a while and then they won't work anymore. Your immune system may be stronger than mine. You have it, Mitch, make no mistake about it."

"I'll throw all of your asses in jail the minute I get out of here. I am not without influence."

"You aren't getting out of here, Senator," Isabelle said. "Caviar, anyone?"

"What the hell does that mean? Kidnapping is against the law. You can't kidnap a United States senator. This scum," he said, jerking his head in the Monarchs' direction, "yeah, but not me."

"Oh, well!" Kathryn said.

Nikki looked down at the stack of quit claim deeds in her hand. "Now, let's tackle those trusts you think you're getting away with. I'm going to need all of your signatures quite a few more times. Shame on you for not mentioning the trusts. I think you were just so agitated you simply forgot."

The women moved toward the door, Isabelle pushing the dolly ahead of her. She closed the door behind her. They all walked down to the end of the hallway.

"We did it! We actually did it! Julia, honey, are you OK?" Alexis asked.

"I'm fine. Did you see his face? I will take that look of disbelief with me forever."

Alexis and Yoko ripped off their black masks. "Now what?" Alexis demanded.

"Charles said we have to dismantle all the

computers," Nikki said. "He won't care if we smash them up. We have to sanitize this place. Charles is working on something for the *Post* and it will hit sometime this week. By then, the four of them will be so far away no one in the world will be able to find them."

"What about all these treasures, the paintings, what's going to happen to them?" Alexis asked.

"They go with the house. Mr. Monarch signed off on everything. Everything will be sold. Charles has it all arranged. Private collectors, you know. We have to take all the money and the jewelry out of the vault and take it to McLean."

"Alexis, you and Yoko take Junior and Senior out to Kathryn's rig. Stick them in the car and use the handcuffs to shackle them to the door handle. Mrs. Monarch gets the passenger seat in front. The senator can bounce around inside the back of the truck for all I care. Tape his hands behind his back and his ankles as well," Nikki said.

Kathryn led Julia over to a brocaded sofa and helped her to stretch out. "Take a nap, Julia. We'll wake you when it's time to leave." Kathryn kissed her cheek and touched her hair with gentle fingers. Julia closed her eyes and was asleep within minutes.

As one, the sisters wiped at their eyes. "Time is money, ladies, let's get to it," Nikki said.

They worked feverishly as they trundled the dolly back and forth to the eighteen-wheeler. It was up to Nikki to sanitize the residence which she did with the air of a professional.

Two hours later, the Monarch mansion was swept clean. Kathryn took a crowbar from the back of her truck and proceeded to smash every machine in the Monarchs' office. The women clapped with enthusiasm. Then they high-fived each other.

Nikki looked around the office. "Charles would be so pleased."

"Did we get everything?" Kathryn asked.

"I went over it twice," Nikki said. "I cleaned out all the other safes on Charles's map and just threw everything in those garbage bags." She held out her hands encased in surgical gloves.

"I'll carry Julia. She's still sleeping. I'll put her in the backseat of the car they arrived in. You're driving her, Nikki. Isabelle will be with Alexis, Yoko and myself. Can you handle it?" Kathryn said.

"Not a problem" Nikki replied. "Be careful, Kathryn, you're carrying some strange cargo this trip. You're going to Baltimore Washington Airport where Charles's people will take over. I'll see you back in McLean."

"See ya!" Kathryn said as she picked up Julia and cradled her to her chest. Her eyes sparkled with unshed tears as she carried her friend out of the house to the car for her ride back to McLean.

"Kathryn, be careful, OK?"

"You know it."

Fourteen

Jack Emery looked down at the bottom of his computer monitor to see the date and the time. Then he fingered his battered face. It was healing much too slowly to suit him. He still wasn't comfortable with the temporary caps on his front teeth. He felt like he had a mouth full of mush that made him lisp when he spoke.

He felt beaten, worn down. Ten long days since he'd been beaten to a pulp. He probably would have starved to death if it hadn't been for Mark and take-out restaurants that delivered. The outside world no longer beckoned. He liked sitting on his chocolate colored sofa watching stupid shows on television and swigging beer from long-neck bottles until he fell asleep. He'd only been out twice, to go to the dentist and to pick up prescriptions.

Jack had no idea what was going on in the outside world. Ten days' worth of newspapers was piled high on his kitchen counter along with ten days' worth of mail. He hadn't turned on a newscast in the same length of time. He knew his old-fashioned answering machine either wasn't working or the little tape was full. He knew this because two red lights glowed on the square black box. One red blinking light meant there were messages, two blinking lights meant the tape was full. It simply did not matter in the scheme of things.

Jack clicked off the computer before he shuffled out to the kitchen and opened the refrigerator. He was stunned to see an array of food filling the shelves. Fresh orange juice, a new container of milk, a new twelve-pack of Bud, apples, cheese, a loaf of bread, lean-looking bacon, a dozen eggs. Cold cuts from a deli in individual plastic bags, hot dogs, some ground beef, cottage cheese, yogurt and salad greens. Mark must have been here during the night. Obviously, he'd tidied up while he was here, too.

Good old Mark. He felt bad that he'd sucked his friend into the mess he'd gotten himself into. He didn't deserve a friend like Mark. Mark agreed. Jack found himself grinning at the thought.

He knew he had to get off his ass and join the

world again. Some world where the bad guys got away with what they were doing and the good guys got the living shit beat out of them. There was something wrong with this picture. Something really wrong.

Jack headed back toward the chocolate colored sofa. Nikki had helped him pick it out, and the day it was delivered, they'd christened it by making love all night long. He looked over at the matching recliner where he liked to tilt back to read the paper. He eyed the sofa but opted for the recliner. His biggest problem right now was what to have for dinner. Maybe chips and salsa or maybe some of the pre-cooked pudding he'd seen in the refrigerator. Both would require little chewing.

Jack propped up his feet and swigged from the Bud. He should go back to work. Back to the grind where he tried to put away the bad guys so some smart-ass defense attorney could lie through his teeth to get his client off so he could do the same damn thing all over again. Where the hell was the justice he'd believed in all his life? Where? He felt like crying but big guys didn't cry. That was a crock. Everything was a crock of crap.

Jack adjusted the volume on the TV set. He watched ten minutes of Montel Williams interviewing defiant, pregnant teenagers before he switched channels. Judge Sophie was railing against some guy who had stiffed his landlord.

He switched channels again to a rerun of *Law and Order* where the good guys made things right in sixty minutes. Another crock. He finally pressed the mute button and reached down into the magazine basket to pull out last month's issue of *Field and Stream*. Maybe he needed to go fishing so he could commune with nature and think about his life. He didn't even know where his fishing pole was. He dropped the magazine back into the basket.

He thought about Nikki because when he came to this point in his daily thinking, memories of her surfaced no matter how hard he tried to block them out. Where was she? What was she doing? The image of her stunned expression when she saw him outside the armory would stay with him to his dying day. He knew then she hadn't known about the beating he suffered. She might not have been privy to the actual details but his gut told him she knew something bad was going to happen. Otherwise . . . why did a doctor and nurse show up so conveniently?

He went back to thinking about what he was going to have for dinner when he heard noise coming from his small foyer. He moved fast, quicker than he'd moved in the last ten days, to the sofa and his gun that was between the cushions. It was in his hand in the blink of an eye, the hammer pulled back. He waited, his heart pounding in his chest.

"It's me, Jack!" Mark called. "Man, it's pouring cats and dogs out there. It took me an hour to get here but I did stop at Mozellie's for some spaghetti and meatballs."

Jack clicked the hammer back into position before he pushed the gun down between the cushions.

"You gotta stop doing this, Mark. I'm not some charity case on your conscience. Tell me how much I owe you so I can square off with you."

"What's a little food between friends? Sorry I haven't been able to get over here more during your waking hours. You were out like a light when I stopped by last night. You look a little better today." All this was said as the FBI agent took out cartons and plastic silverware from the shopping bag that oozed the scent of garlic and parmesan cheese and set everything up on the oversized coffee table. Napkins, little packets of salt, pepper, and a plastic container of grated cheese followed. Mark trotted off to get two fresh bottles of beer. He uncapped both of them. "Dig in, buddy, because this is the best spaghetti and meatballs in the state of Virginia."

As they gobbled their food, they talked baseball and fly fishing. When they were done, Mark tossed everything into the shopping bag along with the empty beer bottles and carried them out to the trash chute in the hallway. The apartment still smelled like garlic and cheese.

The FBI agent and the ADA eyeballed each other from their respective positions. Mark took the initiative and spoke first. "Are you ready to hear about what's going on in the outside world?"

Jack swigged from his bottle. He shrugged. "Not unless it directly affects me. I'm about ready to go back to work. I have a meeting with my boss in two days. Figure if I wear dark glasses, don't smile and try to walk normally, I can pull it off. The truth is, Mark, the job has lost its luster. If it doesn't go well then I'll start looking for a job in the private sector where the pay is a hell of a lot better plus you get a sign-on bonus. How're you doing, buddy?"

"I gave my notice last week. I told you but I guess you don't remember. You were pretty high on pain pills that night. After that visit from those . . . those *shields,* I started looking at things a lot differently. I just couldn't get back into the swing of it. Then they farmed me out to the DOJ and somehow, I screwed up the program. They chewed my ass out and it was the last straw. These last few days I've been busy *correcting* some of the programs I wrote and installed for the Bureau."

"What's that mean?" Jack asked.

"What that means, buddy, is I can access all those programs and no one would ever be the wiser. Same goes for Department of Justice. My codes, my own private back doors, my own fire walls, that kind of thing."

"You sly devil!" Jack said in awe. "Does that mean you're going *private?*"

"What it really means is, *we're* going private. Wait till you hear this. I put up a quickie Web site about ten days ago. I called it the Justice Agency and added a little blurb about righting wrongs, etcetera, etcetera. I applied for grants all over the place under that name and within two days I got a hundred-thousand-dollar-grant from some spinoff of that Monarch HMO set-up. Of course you haven't been reading the papers or listening to the news so you might not know about that. I got the check today. Just like that—a hundred grand. Say something, Jack."

Jack hoisted himself up to a better sitting position. He winced, pain flashing across his face. "Are you telling me Monarch went belly up? If that's the case, how'd you get money out of them?"

"No, no, they didn't go belly up. If you'd read the papers you'd know all about this. It happened a day or so after that armory shindig, after those shields paid us a visit. It was on the front page, above the fold, for about four days. Monarch was private so they could do whatever they wanted. They returned premiums, paid off people whose claims were originally denied. They even printed a list in the paper of the recipients along with apologies. A legal firm in D.C. handled the payouts."

"Which firm?" Jack asked, although he already knew the answer. His hands started to shake.

"Nikki's firm, Jack. Man, think of all those billable hours. Damn, that was a plum for her. There's more. The Monarchs dropped off the face of the earth. No one is looking for them, if that's your next question. And, why should they? They disbanded, got religion, whatever, and decided to right the wrongs the company was responsible for. I have to file reports but that's no big deal. We can keep tabs on Nikki and her firm as well as the others and no one will be the wiser. With my expertise I can hack into her computers anytime I want. Win win, Jack. End of story."

"Why do I feel there's more?" Jack asked uneasily. Dropped off the face of the earth. *Just the way Marie Llewellyn dropped off the face of the earth.*

"Because there is more. Senator Webster and his wife disappeared at the same time. Somehow or other, according to the press, the doctor and the senator got into the wrong limousine and no one has seen them since that night at the armory. The weather was a bitch that night and the senator's detail ended up guarding some elderly Republican couple instead of the Websters. There were some pretty red faces come Sunday morning. The Bureau is on it. Mrs. Webster is gone, too. Seems she had earlier resigned her position at the hospital citing family obligations. As far as I know, no one, and that includes the Bureau, is linking the two together. All five of them literally dropped off the face of the earth. Doesn't say much for the Secret Service, now does it?"

Jack rubbed at the stubble on his bruised and battered face. "I'll be damned."

"So are you in with me or not?"

"That hundred grand isn't going to last very long, Mark."

"Oh, did I forget to tell you, the grant runs for ten years? Ten years, Jack. It will pay us a modest salary, pay the rent on an office plus utilities. We can share an apartment in the beginning to cut down on our personal rent. We're bound to get some clients if we advertise. We can do this, Jack. I can freelance on the side. You gotta resign, though. Can you do that?"

Could he? 'Yeah, I can do that. That means we . . ."

"Yeah, that's what it means, Jack. If we go private we don't have to answer to our bosses and we can play detective all day and all night, twenty-four-seven. And remember this, the mightiest weapon of all is the written word. All we have to do is find some gung ho seasoned reporter who will listen to us, and wait to print the story we give him. When we have a story to give him, that is. I even think I know the right guy, Bob Lyon. They call him The Lion."

"I'm going home now. I suggest your start

reading those newspapers on your kitchen counter and then prepare your resignation letter. You OK?"

"I think I just crossed the threshold to wellness. I expect my recovery to be short of immediate. Should I thank you, kiss your feet, what?"

Mark laughed. "Buy dinner tomorrow night. That means you go out and pick it up. We're gonna get them, Jack."

"Yeah, Mark, we're gonna get *them*." If they don't get us first.

Less than twenty-five miles away, Myra and Charles walked out into the velvet darkness, crystal goblets of wine in hand. They sat down next to one another. Myra reached for his hand and squeezed it before she placed her head on his shoulder.

"It's a beautiful night, isn't it, Charles? It's so quiet. Even the Dobermans are quiet."

"That's because it's midnight," Charles said.

"So it is. We should make a toast, Charles."

"Not yet, dear."

Myra sat up and placed her wine on a rattan table next to the swing she and Charles were sitting in. "Charles, we never speak about . . . about your grief where Barbara is concerned. It's always me wailing. Do you . . . ?"

"No, Myra, I don't. I know you aren't going to understand this and sometimes I don't understand it myself but I just can't . . . I don't know how . . . it's all locked up deep inside me."

Myra patted Charles's hand. "I understand. I didn't think it would ever be possible to love another human being the way I loved Barbara. It's not the same yet it is the same. I think I would lie down and die if anything happened to *our girls.* I pray every night for Julia. I pray for all of them. I hope at some point they can all find happiness. I want so much for all of them. I want Alexis to be able to take her birth name back at some point. I want them all to be whole.

"I wish, Charles, that we could find a way to bring Nikki and Jack together. They were meant for each other. Oh, look, Charles, a shooting star! Quick, make a wish!"

Charles squeezed his eyes shut as did Myra.

"That was me, Mom. How'd you like that?"

Myra's eyes flew open.

Charles bolted off his chair, his eyes wild.

"Whatcha think, Charles? Was that nifty or what?"

"Darling, time to go in, it's getting late."

Myra laughed, the sound ringing across the lawn. "That was the most spectacular shooting star I've ever seen."

"Beyond spectacular," Charles said.

Fifteen

The gorgeous, orange ball in the sky slowly dipped beyond the horizon as the sisters leaned on the railing to watch it disappear.

They were dining by candlelight on the terrace this evening. Even though the table, the retractable, bright colored awning, and the crocks of brilliant flowers were cheerful, the mood was somber. There was no sparkling repartee, no poking one another in fun, no jostling. Even Murphy was subdued, lying on the top step of the stairs that led to the lawn that was greener than any golf course.

The table was set for six instead of the usual eight place settings. The French doors opened as Charles pushed a heavily laden serving cart onto the terrace. He tried to be cheerful when he rattled off the food he would be serving he knew no one was going to eat. He could have served dry shoe leather with ketchup and no one would have noticed or complained. He felt sick to his stomach and there was a knot in his throat as he ladled out food onto the fine china.

Charles watched as the women stirred and mashed and then stirred some more. He was right, no one was eating. Murphy looked up and then ignored what was going on.

"It was a beautiful day today, wasn't it, girls?" Myra said. The others nodded.

Myra tried again. "You all look so beautiful in your summer finery. I do love flower patterned dresses. I think they just make a person feel good." The others nodded.

Myra tried one more time. "Let's all have some cigarettes and beer."

"Now you're talking, Myra," Kathryn said as she got up and beelined for the kitchen. When she came back with a twelve-pack of Corona beer she said, "With a few of these under our belts we'll be able to handle . . . maybe we'll be able . . . shit, never mind."

"I hate beer," Yoko said, as she squeezed lime on the rim of the bottle then upended it. "Where are the cigarettes? I never smoked before."

"And you won't be smoking after tonight either. This is a special occasion. Actually, it's beyond special," Kathryn said fiercely. "Just puff and blow the smoke."

A lot of coughing and sputtering went on to Charles's amusement as he fired up his pipe and leaned back in the springy chair he was sitting on. He didn't know when he'd ever felt this sad, this melancholy. The truth was, he wanted to cry for what was about to happen.

The cicadas sang their song and the night birds chimed in. The old oaks overhead whispered their own song. A faint quarter moon could be seen riding high in a sky sprinkled with millions of stars. The night was deliciously warm but no one seemed to notice.

"I'll have another one of these," Yoko said. "Beer is nothing like tea. I think I like it. Is it mandatory to smoke cigarettes when you drink beer?"

"Yeah, it is," Kathryn said, clapping her on the back. "Drink up. We have another hour to wait."

Twenty-four bottles of beer and two packs of cigarettes later, the women jumped as one when they saw headlights at the security gates. Murphy reared up and then leaped down the steps, raced across the lawn and howled a greeting to Alexis and Julia. Alexis stopped long enough to open the door for Murphy to climb in before she barreled up the drive to come to a screeching halt.

The occupants clustered into a tight knot on

the terrace as they watched the two women follow Murphy. Alexis moved off to the side of the little group to watch the reaction of her sisters.

It was Julia Webster but it wasn't Julia Webster. The woman standing in front of them appeared to be in her late sixties with stooped shoulders, snow white hair and bright blue eyes. She was dressed for traveling in a cream colored suit. Wire rim glasses perched on her nose. She smiled and she was suddenly Julia Webster again. "What do you think? Even I didn't recognize myself when Alexis got through with me. Can I have a beer? I'll take a cigarette, too. By the way, I am now Penelope Tremaine. I have a driver's license, a Visa card, a Master Card, an American Express card and a passport to attest to my new identity, thanks to Charles."

Yoko stumbled all over herself and then giggled as she rushed into the house for more beer and cigarettes. She handed them over with a flourish. "Down the hatch!"

"Don't mind her, she's tipsy," Kathryn said.

"It's a nice memory to take with me." Julia smiled. "Listen, do all of you mind if I take a walk through the house one last time. Alone."

Heads bobbed up and down. Julia moved off, gliding across the terrace and through the open French doors.

Nikki chewed on her lower lip. Kathryn puffed furiously on a cigarette dangling from her lips. Yoko cried openly as Isabelle blew her nose. Myra clung to Charles's arm, her whole body shaking. Charles stared off into the distance as Murphy prowled the terrace from end to end.

"Is she going to be all right or not?" Kathryn growled.

"I don't know, Kathryn. I can't lie to you. The treatment is experimental. It's the only chance she has. We'll know in time."

"She doesn't have time, Charles," Nikki whispered.

"Yes, she does. How much, I can't say. She'll fly through the night and when she arrives in Switzerland, she'll be met by the best team of doctors and nurses in the world. Thanks to Her Majesty. Listen to me now. Even if it kills you, I want smiles. I want cheerful words. I want happiness. I want Julia to leave here with that memory. Do you understand?"

"The car is here, I can see the headlights," Isabelle said.

The sisters turned to see Julia outlined in the doorway. She, too, had seen the headlights. She backed her way into the kitchen. More attuned to Julia than the others, Kathryn dropped her beer and ran into the kitchen to see Julia looking at the plant on the windowsill. She sucked in her breath.

"You better not cry, Julia, or all that shit on

your face is going to melt. The plant's alive. We saved it, and look, it's going to get a new leaf any day now. We gave it life, Julia. You and me."

"Don't let it die, Kathryn. Please."

"I promise. When you get back that plant is going to be as healthy as you will be. That's a Kathryn Lucas promise."

"That's good enough for me. Charles said we could call one another. You'll keep me posted on the plant."

"I will."

"I have to go now. I didn't think this was going to be so hard. What am I going to do without all of you?"

"You're going to be pretty busy, Julia. Go on now so we can all bawl our eyes out." Julia hugged her. Kathryn turned and kissed her on the cheek. "Go on, beat it." She stood at the kitchen window and watched as Julia said her good-byes. She held up until Murphy trotted over to Julia and put his huge paws on her shoulders to balance himself. He nuzzled her neck and growled deep in his throat. Kathryn dropped to her knees, her hands covering her mouth so she wouldn't howl as loud as Murphy.

And then Julia was gone.

Epilogue

Midnight. The witching hour.

Charles took center stage. The others waited for him to speak. They all pretended not to notice how gruff and hoarse his voice was. "I'm optimistic where Julia is concerned. She's going to the right place for her now. Having said that, I suggest we leave Julia's chair empty for now. We're going to take a brief hiatus after we choose the next mission. Does anyone have anything to say before we begin?"

"I do," Nikki said, standing up. "Since you all left it up to me to decide who should get what of the Monarch monies, I made a decision. I awarded a $1.2 million-grant to the Justice Agency. A hundred thousand dollars a year. It's a brand spanking new agency headed up by ex-FBI agent Mark Lane and ex-ADA Jack Emery. If they file all the reports the way they're supposed to, we can keep tabs on them as they are keeping tabs on us. Win win, ladies."

"Bravo, Nikki!" Isabelle said. "I see it now, we're at loggerheads and it's male versus female. We're winning! They're no match for us." Yoko threw a pencil at her.

"It's been a month since . . . since the Monarchs and the senator were spirited away. Is there any news? Are you going to tell us where they are and how they're doing? Did you really send them off wearing loin cloths and . . . whatever that thing was Mrs. Monarch was wearing?" Kathryn asked.

Charles allowed himself a brief smile. "That thing was a muu-muu. I like to think of them as our guests. They are in Africa working on a farm. They get paid twenty-five cents a week. A week, not a day. When they arrived in Africa, they were whisked away to a clinic where all four of them were hypnotized and sent on their way. They believe they belong on the farm and have no recall about their lives here in the States. They will be evaluated from time to time. Their health will be seen to. I understand their appetites are hearty. Their futures have been taken care of. Any other questions?"

"In that case," Myra said, "let's get on with it."

She reached for the shoe box and moved it in front of Nikki. "Choose a name, dear."

Nikki drew in a deep breath and reached for the square of white paper with a printed name on it. She unfolded it, opened it and announced: "Myra."

Myra slumped back in her seat as the others leaped off their chairs to gather around to congratulate her. She was teary eyed as she hugged the women who had become like daughters to her. "Is it really my turn?"

"You bet your sweet bippie it is," Kathryn said.

"Nice going, Nik."

Nikki turned around so she was facing the wall. "Is it OK, Barb?"

"More than OK. See ya upstairs. Willie's waiting for me."

Myra looked up at Nikki and smiled. "It's my turn, Nikki. At last."

Nikki nodded. "We'll do our best to make it come out right, Myra."

"I know that, dear. I know that."

Don't miss any of the novels in
Fern Michaels's thrilling new
Sisterhood series!
Read on for a special excerpt from
WEEKEND WARRIORS
(Kathryn's story), available now.

It was dusk when Nikki Quinn stopped her cobalt-blue BMW in front of the massive iron gates of Myra Rutledge's McLean estate. She pressed the remote control attached to the visor and waited for the lumbering gates to slide open. She knew Charles was watching her on the closed-circuit television screen. The security here at the estate was sophisticated, high-tech, impregnable. The only thing missing was concertina wire along the top of the electrified fence.

Nikki sailed up the half mile of cobblestones to the driveway that led around to the back of the McLean mansion. When she was younger, she and Barbara referred to the house as Myra's Fortress. She'd loved growing up here, loved riding across the fields on Barbara's horse Starlite, loved playing with Barbara in the tunnels underneath the old house that had once been used to aid runaway slaves.

The engine idling, Nikki made no move to get out of the car. She hated coming here these days, hated seeing the empty shell her beloved Myra had turned into. All the life, all the spark had gone out of her. According to Charles, Myra sat in the living room, drinking tea, staring at old photo albums, the television tuned to CNN twenty-four hours a day. She hadn't left the house once since Barbara's funeral.

She finally turned off the engine, gathered her briefcase, weekend bag and purse. Should she put the top up or leave it down? The sky was clear. She shrugged. If it looked like rain, Charles would put the top up.

"Any change?" she asked walking into the kitchen.

Charles shook his head before he hugged her. "She's gone downhill even more these last two weeks. I hate saying this, but I don't think she even noticed you weren't here, Nikki."

Nikki flinched. "I couldn't get here, Charles. I had to wait for a court verdict. I must have called a hundred times," Nikki said, tossing her gear on the countertop. Her eyes pleaded with Myra's houseman for understanding.

Charles Martin was a tall man with clear crystal blue eyes and a shock of white hair that was thick and full. Once he'd been heavier but this past year had taken a toll on him, too. She noticed the tremor in his hand when he handed her a cup of coffee.

"Is she at least talking, Charles?"

"She responds if I ask her a direct question. Earlier in the week she fired me. She said she didn't need me anymore."

"My God!" Nikki sat down at the old oak table with the claw feet. Myra said the table was over three hundred years old and hand-hewn. As a child, she'd loved eating in the kitchen. Loved sitting at the table drinking cold milk and eating fat sugar cookies. She looked around. There didn't seem to be much life in the kitchen these days. The plants didn't seem as green, the summer dishes were still in the pantry, the winter placemats were still on the table. Even the braided winter rugs were still on the old pine floors. In the spring, Myra always changed them. She blinked. "This kitchen looks like an institution kitchen, Charles. The house is too quiet. Doesn't Myra play her music anymore?"

"No. She doesn't do anything anymore. I tried to get her to go for a walk today. She told me to get out of her face. I have to fight with her to take a shower. I'm at my wit's end. I don't know what to do anymore. This is no way to live, Nikki."

"Maybe it's time for some tough love. Let me see if she responds to me this evening. By the way, what's for dinner?"

"Rack of lamb. Those little red potatoes you

like, and fresh garden peas. I made a blackberry cobbler just for you. But when you're not here, I end up throwing it all away. Myra nibbled on a piece of toast today." Charles threw his hands in the air and stomped over to the stove to open the oven door.

Nikki sighed. She straightened her shoulders before she marched into the living room where Myra was sitting on the sofa. She bent down to kiss the wrinkled cheek. "Did you miss me, Myra?"

"Nikki! It's nice to see you. Of course, I missed you. Sit down, dear. Tell me how you are. Is the law firm doing nicely? How's our softball team doing? Are you still seeing that assistant district attorney?" Her voice trailed off to nothing as she stared at the television set whose sound was on mute.

Nikki sat down and reached for the remote control. "I hope you don't mind if I switch to the local station. I want to see the news." She turned the volume up slightly.

"Let's see. Yes, I'm still seeing Jack, and the firm is doing wonderfully. We have more cases than we can handle. The team is in fourth place. I'm fine but I worry about you, Myra. Charles is worried about you, too."

"I fired Charles."

"I know, but he's still here. He has nowhere to go, Myra. You have to snap out of this depression. I can arrange some grief counseling sessions for you. You need a medical checkup. You have to let it go, Myra. You can't bring Barbara back. I can't stand seeing you like this. Barbara wouldn't approve of the way you're grieving. She always said life is for the living."

"I never heard her say any such thing. I can't let it go. She's with me every minute of every day. There's nothing to live for. The bastard who killed my daughter robbed my life as well. He's out there somewhere living a good life. If I could just get my hands on him for five minutes, I would . . ."

"Myra, he's back in his own country. Shhh, listen. That man," Nikki said pointing to the screen, "was set free today because of a technicality. He killed a young girl and he's walking away a free man. Jack prosecuted the case and lost."

"He must not be a very good district attorney if he lost the case," Myra snapped. Nikki's eyebrows shot upward. Was that a spark of interest? Childishly, she crossed her fingers.

"He's an excellent district attorney, Myra but the law is the law. The judge let things go because they weren't legal. Oh, look, there's the mother of the girl. God, I feel so sorry for her. She was in court every single day. The papers said she never took her eyes off the accused, not even for a minute. The reporters marveled at the woman's steadfast intensity. Every day they did an article about her. Jack said she fainted when the verdict came in."

"I know just how she feels," Myra said, leaning

287

forward to see the screen better. "What's she doing, Nikki? Look, there's Jack! He's very photogenic."

Nikki watched as the scene played out in front of her. She saw Jack's lips move, knew he was saying something but she couldn't hear over the voices of the excited news reporters. She saw his arm reach out but he was too late. Marie Lewellen fired the gun in her hand point-blank at the man who killed her daughter.

The television screen turned black and then came to life again.

Barnes looked directly into the camera, his eyes wide with shocked disbelief. Blood bubbled from his mouth. "I . . . should have . . . killed . . . you, too . . . you bitch!"

"You killed my little girl. You don't deserve to live. I'm glad I killed you. Glad!" Marie Lewellen screamed.

Barnes fell face forward onto the concrete steps of the courthouse.

Chaos erupted but the camera stayed positioned, capturing the ensuing panic.

"Oh my God!" was all Nikki could say.

Myra reared back against the cushions. "Did you see that! That's what I should have done! I hope she killed the son of a bitch! Is he moving? I can't see. Is he dead, Nikki? Charles, come see this. Why didn't I have the guts to do what that woman just did?" Myra shouted, her skinny arms flailing up and down. "If she killed him, I want you to defend her, Nikki. I'll pay for everything. Use your whole firm. Every expert, every specialist in the world. She killed him. She got in his face and killed him. Tell me he's dead. I want to know if he's dead!"

Nikki looked at Charles, who was busy staring at the ceiling. "He's dead, Myra."

"Look, look! They're handcuffing her. They're going to take her to jail. I want you to leave right now. Post her bail, do something. Don't let them keep her in jail. Say you'll take her home with you. Tell them she won't be a menace to society. Charles, get my checkbook."

"Myra, for God's sake, simmer down. It's not that easy."

"The hell it isn't. She was crazed. Temporary insanity. Are you going to do it or not, Nikki?"

"Yes, but . . ."

"Don't give me buts. You're still sitting here. I never asked you to do a thing for me, Nikki. Never once. I'm asking you now."

"I didn't say I wouldn't do it, Myra. I need to think. I need to talk to Jack. I can have my paralegal go down to the station. Tomorrow morning will be time enough. There is no way in hell she's getting out of jail tonight. She has to be arraigned. Can you wait for morning, Myra?"

"Yes, I can wait for morning." Myra swung around. "Charles, did you see what that woman just did?

I would cheerfully rot in prison if I had the guts to do that. First thing in the morning, Nikki. I want you to call me with a full report."

"You don't answer the phone, Myra," Nikki said sourly.

"I'll answer it tomorrow. Isn't it time for dinner? Let's eat off trays this evening. I want to see what happens to that poor woman. They'll be reporting on this for hours. Does she have other children? A husband? Isn't anyone going to answer me?"

Nikki's jaw dropped. Charles spun around on his heel, a smirk on his face.

"I can tell you what Jack told me. She has two other children, and yes, she has a husband. She's a homemaker. She works at a Hallmark shop on weekends for extra money that goes for all the little extras young kids need. Her husband is a lineman for AT&T. Her two boys are nine and eleven. Jenny, the daughter that was killed, worked after school till closing at the same Hallmark shop. She had a flat tire the night she was killed. She was fixing it herself when that creep offered to help, and then he snatched her and dumped her body out near Manassas. Jack said they're a very nice family. Marie went to PTA meetings and they went to church as a family on Sunday."

"They'll need someone to take care of the boys, to cook and do all the things a mother does in case they don't let her out right away.

Charles, find someone for the family. Use that employment agency we use when we do our spring cleaning. I hope they give her a medal. Someone should."

"Myra, for God's sake, she killed a man in cold blood. She took the law into her own hands. Civilized people don't do things like that. That's why we have laws."

"Where was the law when that bastard killed my daughter? Did Barbara get justice? No, she did not! My daughter is dead and no one paid for that crime. My unborn grandchild is dead and no one paid for that crime either. I'll go to my grave never having seen my grandchild. Don't talk to me about justice. Don't talk to me about the law because I don't want to hear it. Those laws, the justice that freed that man . . . *suck*."

Nikki looked up to see Charles standing in the doorway. She watched as both his clenched fists shot upward. In spite of herself, she grinned. Myra was alive and belching fire. All she had to do was get her to calm down and maybe, just maybe, she would return to the land of the living.

It was midnight when Jack Emery finally returned Nikki's call. She crawled into bed, her head buzzing with the evening's events.

"Did you see it, Nikki?"

"Of course I saw it. Myra and Charles saw it,

too. I'll say one thing, it snapped Myra out of her fugue. At least for now. She wants me to defend Marie Lewellen. I said I would."

"You can't defend her. It's open and shut. Insanity isn't going to hold up. She admitted to buying the gun at lunchtime from some punk on the street. That goes to premeditation. They've charged her with first degree murder. I'll be prosecuting, Nikki."

"Pass on it, Jack. You did enough to that woman."

"What the hell is that supposed to mean, Nikki?"

"It means that asshole got off. That's exactly what it means, Jack. Myra was right when she said it sucked. You didn't fight hard enough. He was guilty as sin and you damn well know it."

"The judge threw out . . . why am I defending myself? I did the best job I could under the circumstances. I tried to stop her at the courthouse. I was seconds too late. Don't go sour on me now. Turn it over to someone else in your firm, Nikki."

"I can't do that, Jack. I promised Myra. She's never, ever, asked anything of me. I have to do what she wants. I'm going to give you the fight of your life, too."

"If you take this case on that means we aren't going to be able to see one another until it's over, at which point we'll probably hate each other's guts. Is that what you want?"

Nikki's mind raced. No, it wasn't what she wanted but she knew where her loyalties lay. She loved Jack Emery. "Beg off, Jack. Let some other A.D.A. take the case."

"I guess I'll see you in court, Counselor," Jack said coldly.

It was his tone, not his words, that sparked her reply. "You bet your sweet ass you'll see me in court." Nikki snapped her cell phone shut and threw it across the room.

Nikki punched at the thick downy pillows. She knew she wasn't going to be able to sleep now. She felt like crying. A second later she bounded out of the twin bed and ripped down the covers from the bed that once belonged to Barbara. If she wanted to, she could stick her hand under the pillow and pull out Barb's old beat-up teddy bear and hug it to her chest the way Barb had done every night she slept in the bed. It almost seemed sacrilegious to touch it. Instead she picked up the pillow and looked down at the tattered bear named Willie. She almost stuck her finger in the hole under Willie's chin but changed her mind. She lowered the pillow and went back to her own bed. Tears rolled down her cheeks. "God, I miss you, Barb. I think about you every day. I just had a fight with Jack. At least I think it was a fight. I wish you were here so I could call you up and tell you all about it." She punched at the down pillows again. Maybe she needed to read herself to sleep. Her gaze traveled to the built-in book-shelves across the room. The three top shelves were hers because she was taller than Barbara. The three bottom shelves belonged to Barbara and were loaded with everything *but* books. No, she was too wired-up to read.

The first month she'd come here to live, Myra had knocked out two walls and turned this room into a two-girl bedroom. They'd spent so many hours in here, huddled in their beds, gig-gling, telling secrets, talking about boys and sharing all their hopes and dreams. Even the bath-room had twin vanities and twin showers. Myra didn't stint and she didn't favor one over the other. She simply had enough love for both of them. She looked now at the twin desks, the col-orful swivel chairs, the bright red rocking chairs. It seemed so long ago, almost like a lifetime. She stared at the colorful rockers and at the cush-ions they'd made at camp one year. Barbara's was perfect, her stitches small and neat. Her own was sloppy, the seams loose. But it wasn't the cushions that held her gaze. The chair was rock-ing, moving slowly back and forth. She looked up to see if the fan was on. A chill washed down her spine. She shuddered as she reached for her robe. Maybe Charles had left some coffee in the pot. If not, she could make some more.

Nikki walked down the long hallway to the back staircase that led to the kitchen. She blinked when she saw Myra and Charles sitting at the table, highball glasses in their hands. She blinked again. "I couldn't sleep," she mumbled.

"We couldn't either," Myra said.

"After what we saw on television this evening, I can understand why. I'm going to make some coffee."

"Nikki, Charles and I want to talk to you about something."

Nikki reached for the coffee canister. There was an edge to Myra's voice. A combative edge. Something she'd never heard before. "About what, Myra? I said I would take Marie Lewellen's case."

"I know. That's just a small part of it. Do you remember a while back when you told Charles and myself about two young women who came to see you? Kathryn Lucas and Alexis Thorne, only that wasn't Alexis Thorne's real name at the time?"

"I remember," Nikki said, measuring coffee into the stainless steel basket.

"You helped Alexis by going outside the law. You couldn't help Kathryn because the statute of limitations had run out, but if there was a way to help her, would you do it?"

Nikki felt herself freeze. "Are you talking about inside the law or outside the law, Myra?"

"Don't answer my question with a question. Would you help her?"

"I can't, Myra. There's nothing I can do for her. I looked at everything. Time ran out. Yes, I feel sorry for her. I understand how it all went down. She waited too long, that's the bottom line."

"You looked the other way for Alexis. You knew someone who was on the other side of the law and you got her a new identity, you helped her start a small home business as a personal shopper and you made it happen for her. You believed in her when she told you her story. She was a victim, she didn't deserve to go to prison for a whole year. She can never get that year of her life back. The men and women who turned her into a scapegoat walked free and are living the good life and her life is ruined. Kathryn is a victim and no one is helping her. Marie Lewellen could spend the rest of her life in jail unless you can get her off. Legally."

Nikki sat down across from Myra and Charles. "I think this would be a real good time for you to tell me *exactly* what you two are talking about."

"The system you work under doesn't always work," Charles said.

"Sometimes that's true," Nikki said carefully. "For the most part, it works."

Myra looked at Nikki over the rim of her glass. "What if we take the part that doesn't work and make it work? What if I told you I was willing to use my entire fortune, and you know, Nikki, that it is sizeable, and use it to . . . make that system work. For us. For all the Maries, the Kathryns and the Alexis Thornes who got lost in the system."

"Are you talking about going outside the law to . . . to . . . avenge these women? Are you talking about taking the law into your own hands and . . . and . . ."

Myra's head bobbed up and down. "Charles can help. He dealt with criminals and terrorists during his stint at MI6. You're an attorney, a law professor. With your brains, Charles's expertise and my money, we could right quite a few wrongs. It would have to be secret, of course."

"And you just now came up with all this?" Nikki said in awe. "No!"

"Yes," Myra and Charles said in unison.

Nikki looked at her watch. "Just eight hours ago, give or take a few minutes, you were practically comatose, Myra. You didn't want to live. You were so deep in your misery and your depression I wanted to cry for you. Now you're all set to take on the judicial system and dispense your own brand of justice. You'll get caught, Myra. You're too old to go to jail. They aren't kind to old people in jail. NO!"

Myra took a long pull from the highball glass. "If I can't satisfy my own vengeance, maybe I can do something for others where the system failed." She spoke in a low, even monotone. "Kathryn Lucas, age thirty-eight. Married to Alan Lucas, the love of her life. Alan had multiple sclerosis as well as Parkinson's disease and lived in a wheelchair. They owned an eighteen-wheeler, Alan's dream. In order to keep his dream alive for him, Kathryn drove the rig and Alan rode alongside her. One night when they stopped for food and gas, Kathryn was raped at a truck stop by three bikers. Alan was forced to watch and could not help his wife. Rather than report the rape and destroy what was left of her husband's manhood, she remained silent. She did nothing. She carried it with her day and night for the next seven years until Alan died. Needless to say, whatever was left of the marriage after the rape, died right then and there. The day after she buried her husband she went to you, gave you all the information she had on the case and you turned her away because the stupid statute of limitations had run out. You told me she had a partial license plate, her husband took pictures, and she said one of the bikers was riding an old Indian motorcycle. You said she told you they belonged to the Weekend Warriors club, probably white-collar professionals out for a fling. Charles said there aren't many Indians in existence and they're on every biker's wish list. It shouldn't be hard to track it down. You just sit there, Nikki, and think about three men raping you while Jack is forced to watch. You think about that."

"Myra, I don't have to think about it. I feel terrible for Kathryn Lucas. Yes, she deserves to have something done but she waited too long. The law is the law. I'm a goddamn lawyer. I can't break the law I swore to uphold."

"The circumstances have to be brought into consideration. I need you to help us, Nikki."

"What is it you want me to do?"

"We could form this little club. You certainly know plenty of women who have slipped through the cracks. Like Alexis, Kathryn, and many others. We'll invite them to join and then we'll do whatever has to be done."

Nikki stood up and threw her hands in the air. "You want us to be *vigilantes!*"

"Yes, dear. Thank you. I couldn't think of the right word. Don't you remember those movies with Charles Bronson?"

"He got caught, Myra."

"But they let him go in the end."

"It was a damn movie, Myra. Make-believe. You want us to do the same thing for real. Just out of curiosity, supposing we were able to find the men that raped Kathryn Lucas, what would we do to them?"

Myra smiled. "That would be up to Kathryn now, wouldn't it?"

"I don't believe I'm sitting here listening to you two hatch this . . . this . . . what the hell is it, Myra?"

"A secret society of women who do what has to be done to make things right," Myra said solemnly.

"It could work, Nikki, as long as we hold to the secrecy part," Charles said quietly. "There is that room in the tunnels where you and Barbara used to play. You could hold your meetings there. No one would ever know. I know exactly how to set it all up."

Nikki struggled for a comeback that would make sense. In the end, she said, "Jack Emery will be prosecuting Marie Lewellen. We'll be adversaries."

"I see," Myra said. She slapped her palms on the old, scarred tabletop. "Then you have to get her out on bail and we'll find a way to whisk her and her family away to safety. I have the money to do that. It will be like the Witness Protection Program. Charles can handle all that."

Nikki sat down with a thump. "If I don't agree to . . . go along with this, what will you do?"

Myra borrowed a line from her favorite comedian. "Then we'll have to kill you," she said cheerfully. "So, are you in?"

"God help me, I'm in."

Here is an excerpt from
another Sisterhood book,
VENDETTA,
which is Myra's story,
now available
wherever books are sold.

Myra walked over to the kitchen door to peer outside. She eyed the temperature gauge and gasped. "Charles, it's twenty-seven degrees! Good heavens! Do we have enough wood for all the fireplaces? We did have an oil delivery, didn't we? We're going to freeze down in the war room."

"Darling, relax. We have two full cords of wood. I carried several loads in earlier this afternoon. Oil was delivered three days ago. We are not going to freeze. Don't you remember, dear, we had special heaters installed in the war room in early September?"

"You're right, I forgot. I am just so overwhelmed that I am finally . . . Never mind, it's all I've been talking about today. Your ears must be sore by now. The girls are late, aren't they?"

"No, Myra, the girls are not late. We said seven and it's only six-thirty. Please try and relax. Do you think they will like my dinner? I thought about doing something fancy and elegant but decided that, with the weather, the girls might like some comfort food. And I know how you like my pot roast."

"It smells wonderful, Charles. The potato pancakes are my favorite. We have both sour cream and apple sauce, right?"

Charles wagged his wooden spoon in the air. "I have it all under control, right down to the wine, salad and dessert—and no, I did not forget Murphy."

"Oh, Charles, whatever would I do without you? Never mind, I don't even want to think about that. They're *almost* late."

"Almost doesn't count, my dear." Charles pointed to the security monitor positioned over the back door. "I think they're here now. I see Kathryn's rig in the lead. I think they wait at the end of the road so they can all arrive at the same time."

"I think so, too. One car is missing, Charles. The girls will want to know all about Julia." Myra started to fret again. "It's not going to be the same without her. The empty chair is going to . . . Oh, Charles, I feel like crying."

"There's no time to cry, Myra. I hear Murphy barking. I think that means he's glad to be back.

Open the door, welcome our guests. We'll talk about Julia later."

There were squeals of delight, backslapping, high-fives and hugs galore as the five women and Murphy raced into the kitchen. The jabbering was so high-pitched that Murphy went into the huge family room to lie by the fireplace.

"Oh, I missed you all," Isabelle said happily.

Alexis dumped her red bag by the door and ran to Myra. She hugged her so hard, Myra squealed for mercy. Yoko, always subdued, clapped everyone on the back and then hugged them all. Kathryn ran around the counter to the kitchen window to see if Julia's plant was still there. It was.

"Oh, God. Oh, God, it has two new leaves! Hey, everyone, Julia's plant has two new leaves! We have to move it, Myra. It's too cold on the windowsill. See how the leaves are limp. Where can I put it? Yoko, you're the plant expert, what should we do?"

The women crowded around to stare at the plant Julia had left behind when she went to Switzerland, hoping to find a cure for her deadly disease. Myra looked stricken, as though she had somehow personally failed their missing sister.

Yoko picked up the plant, stuck her finger in the soil and then touched the leaves. "Some light, a little warmer area and it will be fine," she said.

It was finally decided to place the little plant on a small folding table directly under the kitchen skylight. Everyone sighed with relief.

"Any news about Julia?" Nikki asked as she filched a strip of bacon that was to go into the arugula salad. Charles pretended to swat her with his wooden spoon.

"Julia is doing well," Charles said. "She's gained eight pounds in the last four months. She's tolerating her meds and she misses us all terribly. She's coming home for Thanksgiving, and again for Christmas, but then will go back for another six months. What that means is that she's holding her own and she has not regressed or gotten worse. She's happy. She reads, takes walks, rides her bicycle. Her stamina is better than it's ever been. I spoke to her yesterday. She misses you all and she sends her love. She wants you to give Murphy a big hug for her. The first thing she asked about was the plant. To say she was over-joyed at the two new leaves would be putting it mildly." This last comment was addressed to Kathryn, who was busily wiping tears from the corners of her eyes.

"Everything smells wonderful," Nikki said as she carried candles and napkins into the dining room. "Anything new these past few weeks?" she asked Myra.

"Nothing, dear. Charles and I have just been rattling around out here all by ourselves. No one has called or stopped by. Is there any news on Jack?"

"No. That's why I thought . . . I assumed he would. . . . Damn, I don't know what I thought or assumed. I check his and Mark's new website daily. I have no clue what the two of them are doing. That could be good or it could be bad."

"I can't believe Jack gave up his job as assistant district attorney, and I can't believe his friend would give up his job as a federal agent just like that," Isabelle said.

"Well, he did." Nikki clicked a lighter to light the scented candles. Within seconds the room smelled like blueberries.

"Are we celebrating something special tonight?" Yoko asked.

"Yes. The good news on Julia, your arrival and anything else we want to celebrate," Myra said. "Goodness, how I've missed you all. But before I forget, Charles and I want to invite you all for Thanksgiving, Christmas and New Year's. Please say you will come."

"You bet," Kathryn said.

"Wouldn't miss it for the world," Alexis said.

"I will be glad to attend," Yoko said. "My husband will spend the day sleeping so he will not miss me."

Isabelle and Nikki smiled and nodded.

"We go out to the woods and chop the tree down," Myra said. "If it snows, we pull the tree on a sled, but if there's no snow we pull it on a wagon. We cut all the evergreens the same day so they'll be fresh. We haven't really celebrated Christmas here at Pinewood for some years now. I think it's time to get back to our traditions."

"Christmas here at Pinewood is a marvel. The house smells heavenly with all the balsam," Nikki said. "The vaulted ceiling allows us to have a twenty-foot tree and balsam twined around the bannister going all the way to the second floor. Lots of red velvet bows and our own mistletoe. Myra always made it like a fairyland for Barbara and me. One year, Lu Chow, Myra's gardener, played Santa. She thought we wouldn't notice a Chinese Santa. We pretended not to for her sake."

"You knew? You little rascal!" Myra said. Nikki laughed.

They could have been simply a group of young people getting together to play catch-up, or possibly a group of old friends enjoying dinner together.

"I had a date!" Kathryn blurted out, her face rosy pink. She looked around the table at the stunned looks.

"Tell me you didn't wear that flannel shirt and those Frye boots," Alexis said.

"No, I didn't wear them. I got dressed up. Pantyhose, makeup, the whole magilla."

"And?" the others chorused as one.

"And nothing. Murphy didn't like him. By

the end of the evening he was all over me. I had to deck him, at which point he got a little pissy with me. He was so good-looking he made my eyes water. But I won't be seeing him again. Now, don't ask me any questions because I told you the whole thing."

"I had a date, too," Alexis said. "One of the women I shop for fixed me up with her next-door neighbor. Nice guy. He manages La Belle, that new restaurant in D.C. The food was excellent. He asked me out again. I said yes." Everyone clapped their approval.

"I bought a plasma TV," Nikki said.

"I had to get a new transmission for my car," Isabelle said.

"Well, nothing is new in my life," Yoko said. "I ordered two thousand poinsettias for the holidays. With Lu Chow helping us I will be able to get away for your mission, Myra. I owe you many thanks for allowing him to work at odd times for us. My husband likes him very much."

"That leaves you, Charles. Share with us what you've been up to," Kathryn said.

Charles chuckled. "I've been trying to amuse Myra because she missed you all so much. In my free time I've been working on the details of her mission."

"Guess that means we're all caught up. Let's clear up this mess," Nikki said, waving at the table, "so we can get down to business."

* * *

The war room, as they called it, was warm and cozy. Computer monitors lined the walls, along with television monitors tuned to the three major cable networks: CNN, MSNBC and Fox. Directly in the women's line of vision was an oversized monitor showing the scales of justice, with Lady Justice looking down on them.

A soft whirring could be heard above the quiet tones on the televisions. A fortune in the latest high-tech equipment was at Charles's fingertips. Some of the equipment was so advanced even the FBI didn't have it. "Spare no expense, get the best so the girls are kept safe," Myra had said. And Charles had done just that. He was Lord Supreme in this room and everyone knew it.

Myra usually presided over the meetings, but as it was her mission that was to be discussed this evening, Nikki rose and addressed the group.

"This is where we all give input after Myra tells us what she wants done to the man who killed Barbara. We all know he's back in China and that's our first hurdle. I personally don't see any way to entice him back here, so that means we have to go there. We'll have to figure out a way to do that, of course. First, though, I think Myra might want to say something. Myra, the floor is yours," Nikki said, sitting down.

Myra stood up, her legs wobbly. She grasped

the edge of the table with both hands as she stared around at the women who were now like daughters to her. They were her family and she knew that, no matter what she asked of them, they would do it, if humanly possible. How much should she ask of them? Going to a foreign country to seek her vengeance seemed extreme. Still, there really was no other way to punish her daughter's killer. She looked from one to the other, recognizing each one's particular strength. If anyone could help her, it was these five beautiful, talented women.

Myra licked at her dry lips. "I . . . My justice is going to be dangerous to all of you. I don't know if I have the courage to ask you to . . . to help me. I won't be offended if you want to opt out of my mission. Somehow, some way, I'll get justice for my daughter. What I'm trying to say is, if anything happened to any of you, I wouldn't be able to live with myself. This won't be anything like Kathryn's or Julia's missions.

"You all know Charles's background, and we'll be operating in his field of expertise. But none of you are Charles and none of you are like the operatives he worked with when he was in Her Majesty's service. Right away, that puts us all at a disadvantage."

Kathryn, always the most vocal of the group, squawked her displeasure at what Myra was saying. "Myra, Myra, you're forgetting something. We're *women*! That alone gives us an edge! I rest my case." Everyone cheered, including Charles. Myra grinned from ear to ear.

"Well said, Kathryn. You are forgiven, dear. How stupid of me to forget women can do anything they set their minds to. I think I might be a little overwhelmed at this point. Now, let's decide how we are going to take care of Mr John Chai, my daughter's killer."

"If Julia was here, she could do a little slice and dice with a *very* dull knife. But since she isn't here, I'll volunteer to do the honors, and if he bleeds to death, oh, well," Alexis said.

"That's too good for him. He needs to suffer. His father needs to suffer for protecting him. Let's see what Charles has come up with."

Charles shuffled through the papers in front of him. When he had them in order, images appeared on the screen as Lady Justice faded away. "This is John Chai." A second picture appeared. "This is Chai Ming, China's former Ambassador to the United States. He is retired now and living in Hong Kong. From what I've been able to garner from my sources, Chai Ming has a pretty tight rein on his playboy son." Charles sought Myra's eye. "I haven't been able to find any evidence of employment of any kind. I would assume he's living off the largesse of his father, Chai Ming. John's Harvard education was a waste."

"Is he still covered under the law of diplomatic immunity even though his father is retired?" Yoko asked.

"Yes, but he cannot return to the United States for fear of reprisals, that sort of thing. It's obvious the man stays close to home under his father's supervision. Sooner or later, he's going to wander off the reservation. It's a given that he will not return here to America. That means we will bring him here. Unwillingly, of course."

The women gasped as one. "You mean we're going to go to China and . . . and . . ."

"Snatch the son of a bitch?" Kathryn said. "Yep, that's what it means all right."

"Tell us how we are going to get inside China, snatch this guy, and get back out," Nikki demanded. "I would think the Chai family are watched as closely as our Secret Service agents watch over our retired politicians."

Charles nodded. "You're right, Nikki, but in China they are watched even more closely. I can't swear to this, but I do know how the Chinese think in these matters. It's doubtful Ming's own eye is on his son. There are hundreds of eyes on him. They don't want any kind of scandal that will make them lose face. Family is very important. Respect of one's family is paramount."

Myra's eyes pooled with tears. "If it's impossible, why are we even discussing the matter? Why was I so foolish to think we could finally get to . . . that . . . hellish person?"

"Myra, dear, it is not impossible to get to John Chai. However, it will be a very dangerous and difficult mission for all of us. We are going to need a lot of outside help."

"What kind of help?" Isabelle asked nervously.

"Chinese help. In . . . ah . . . in my other life, I made friends with some very unlikely people. People that I was forced to depend on to stay alive. One develops, over time, instincts where people are concerned. I have a friend named Su Zhow Li. He got me out of a rather horrid situation and then I was able to save his life later on. He is probably in his mid-seventies by now if he is still alive. I haven't been able to renew old friendships since moving here. That was one of the conditions of my transfer from England to America. I'm now willing to ignore that condition.

"Li was born in China but spent many years living in England. His father was British, his mother came from a very well-to-do Chinese family. In the early fifties, as some of you may know, China undertook a massive economic and social reconstruction program. China's new leaders curbed inflation by restoring the economy, and rebuilt many of its war-damaged industrial plants." It had been years since Li told him this story, and Charles wondered if he was remembering everything correctly.

"China's new leaders, with their new-found authority, wedged their way into almost every phase of Chinese life. It worked for a few years, then Mao Zedong, founder of the People's Republic, broke away from the Soviet model of Communism and announced what he thought of as an even better economic system. They called it the Great Leap Forward. The goal was to raise industrial and agricultural production. They formed communes. People had factories in their back yards. It was disastrous because the normal market mechanisms were disrupted, and so agricultural production fell behind. The Chinese people exhausted themselves by producing what later turned out to be shoddy goods that were not fit for sale."

"Tell me about it," Yoko grumbled. "I wouldn't buy something that said "made in China" for all the tea in China." She giggled at her witticism.

"Bad timing, poor planning, whatever you want to call it, the Chinese people were starving. Around this time, Li's family sought passage to his father's homeland."

Charles knew he'd piqued the women's interest when Kathryn asked, "How did they manage to get out of China?"

Charles grinned wryly. "Very carefully, that's how. Li never gave me all the details, but he did say it was a long, dangerous journey. Li's mother had connections and money. They finally arrived in England and amassed a fortune in silks. Li was sent to America and graduated from Harvard at the top of his class. He is a brilliant man. Years and years later, he returned to Hong Kong a very wealthy man."

"Is he going to help us?" Nikki asked.

"Patience, my dear, patience," Charles said.

Myra banged her clenched fist on the table. "I have no patience, Charles. Please, get to the point. Do you have a plan?" Her tone of voice said quite clearly that Charles *had better have* a plan.

Evidently Charles thought so, too. "The reason I brought up my old friend Li is because he has a private airstrip outside of Hong Kong."

The silence in the room was palpable as the women digested Charles's words. That brought it all front and center. They were going to China.

"I'm waiting for Li to contact me via a scrambled phone. I'll have more details as soon as I hear from him." Charles looked around at the sisters. They all looked worried, except Myra who was smiling serenely. "This . . . caper . . . will test your skills to the fullest."

"Like hacking off three guys' balls didn't take skill!" Kathryn hooted, referring to their first mission. The others clapped their hands in agreement. "And let's not forget those creeps we just sent off to Africa. Skill is knowing what to do at precisely the right moment. As women we have a honed instinct that allows us to improvise in a heartbeat."

The women clapped again. Myra clapped the loudest, her eyes bright and shiny.

Books by Bestselling Author
Fern Michaels

Romantic Suspense from
Lisa Jackson

More by Bestselling Author

Lori Foster